THE GAUNTLET

An Encyclopocalypse Reissue

The first rounds shattered the glass of the bedroom window and splashed through the flimsy curtains, imbedding themselves in the plaster walls with powdery explosions.

Shockley heard the echoes of shots striking all through the house.

The empty bathroom. She got out of there somehow.

There was no exit. But somehow…

Another barrage slammed into the old house, deafening him. Bullets gouged away at rotten wood and ricocheted off interior walls and fixtures; bulbs shattered; electric wires split under the plaster hissed and sparked; doors splintered.

It was a cacophony straight from hell. Shockley, helpless, terrified, found release in a bellow of primal despair:

"MAAALLLYYY!"

Tear gas canisters rocketed into the bedroom, discharging their noxious fumes with muffled *whumps,* the smoke-like gas curling into the air like thick swamp mist and obscuring the view of the bed where only minutes before Shockley had lain enjoying the gentle caresses of a woman, where he had lain in complete, calculating control of the whole situation.

But now he was cornered game…

A novel by MICHAEL BUTLER & DENNIS SHRYACK
based on their original screenplay

A Malpasso Production
for Warner Bros. Starring

CLINT EASTWOOD

Produced by ROBERT DALEY
Directed by CLINT EASTWOOD

Now with a new introduction by MICHAEL BUTLER

THE GAUNTLET

Encyclopocalypse Publications
www.encyclopocalypse.com

An Encyclopocalypse Book

Based on the motion picture *The Gauntlet*.

Cover design by Amanda Dempsey.

Interior layout and design by Mark Alan Miller.

First Encyclopocalypse paperback edition, 2026.

Published by arrangement with Michael Butler and Jennifer Shryack.

Printed in the United States of America.

ISBN: 978-1-966037-64-4

This book is dedicated to the memory of Dennis R. Shryack,
beloved husband, esteemed collaborator,
gifted storyteller, ace freshwater fisherman.

You took 'em home, Den.

M.B.

THE GAUNTLET

FOREWORD

From 1972 through 1985, with a few interruptions, the late Dennis Shryack and I were writing partners. The third script we wrote together – an original screenplay – was *The Car*. We wrote it in 14 days and our agent sold it in 48 hours for $250,000. It took us a little longer to write our next "original" and we had no idea that it would become an even stronger follow-up. We called it *The Gauntlet*.

Screenwriting has been in the Butler DNA for a hundred years. My grandfather, Frank Butler, won an Oscar for *Going My Way*; my maternal grandmother created an enduring movie character named Andy Hardy, and my screenwriter parents, Hugo Butler and Jean Rouverol, were riding the wave of professional success until the HUAC witch-hunt and resulting Blacklist left us with no practical choice but to emigrate to Mexico City in 1951, together with Dalton Trumbo and his family. Trumbo (as everyone called him) had recently completed a twelve-month term in prison as one of the "Hollywood Ten" who disputed the HUAC's legitimacy. The next ten years would see his screenplays win two Oscars.

I wrote my first screenplay in 1963. It was optioned by the cinematographer-director Haskell Wexler but never produced (although I did receive an associate producer credit on his 1969 milestone *Medium Cool*). For several years my closest friend from childhood, Trumbo's son Chris and I were a writing team, cutting our teeth in TV on *The Most Dangerous Game* and *Bearcats* for David Friedkin and Mort Fine. Then, on assignment, we wrote six episodes of *Ironside*. Soon we landed a movie assignment: writing *The Don is Dead* for Hal Wallis, whose body of work included *Casablanca, The Maltese Falcon, True Grit* and nearly a dozen Elvis movies.

It may not have been our best work (or Mr. Wallis's), but we were hired by David Gerber to create the Robert Forster TV series *Nakia*. It was well-reviewed but only lasted for a single season. It led to our writing the screenplay *Brannigan* for Levy-Gardner-Laven. The picture was our first moderate feature film success, and the irony of arch-conservative GOP icon John Wayne hiring the sons of famously Blacklisted "reds" wasn't lost on us. In our estimation, The Duke was a prince.

Following another assignment with Levy-Gardner-Laven and a lavish option of an original screenplay (*The Bull*) to Robert Mulligan, Chris and I went our separate ways. Between a handful of writing gigs on *Baretta,* I found another writing partner in Dennis Shryack. Dennis had been a junior agent at Eisenbach-Greene-Duchow (which represented me); he had a couple of movie credits under his belt as well as a tremendous knack for story ideas and commercial narrative. The first script we wrote together was called *Two Weeks with Pay* – the saga of two military-industrial work bros who take a camper vacation into the desert, where their friendship devolves into a two-man *Lord of the Flies*.

I was in a different desert on the set of *Electra Glide in Blue*, doing a dialogue polish for Robert Blake (and playing the film's hapless trucker), when I got word that *Two Weeks* was being optioned by Robert Aldrich. Bob had directed huge hits: *Autumn Leaves* (quietly written by my parents during the Blacklist), *The Dirty Dozen*, and *The Longest Yard*. And though *Two Weeks* was a compelling screenplay, Bob never made the movie. Maybe someday someone will.

Unlike *The Car*, which we rolled out in two weeks, writing *The Gauntlet* took us nine months. The steps of our process had become a pattern by then. This time it was Dennis who came up with the premise: a down and out Phoenix cop gets picked by someone high up in the PD to go to Las Vegas and bring back a witness – some two-bit punk. What the cop isn't told is that this witness' testimony can establish a link between the Police Commissioner and a Vegas mob boss.

In short, the not-too-bright cop has been set up to fail. It was an irresistible idea – a tad more interesting, I thought, if the witness were a woman, sassy and sexy: a prostitute with a college degree. Seeing the value of this approach, Dennis wrote an opening page to give me his sense of the main character, Ben Shockley. I wrote a rough draft and Dennis wrote a revision, then, together, we wrote a subsequent draft: Blakelock became the head of IA rather than Police Commissioner; Shockley's scene with the bikers became a bravura set piece, but... there was still something missing.

"Here's what I think we need," Dennis said. "I want you to do two page of pure writing that describes how it feels inside the bus as the entire Phoenix police department is shooting at them."

This exercise helped us tighten the bond between Ben Shockley and Augustina Mally, defining them as flesh-and-blood characters with whom the movie's audience might resonate. When we finally wrote the words *"FADE OUT"* we felt we had a well-crafted screenplay.

Our agent, Harold Greene, made fifty copies of the script and papered the town with them, much as he'd done with *The Car* eighteen months earlier. Within thirty-six hours we heard that Barbra Streisand wanted to star in *The Gauntlet* –

and direct it too. Hardly a day later we heard that Clint Eastwood also wanted to direct and star in it. For a few minutes it appeared as if they *both* might be in it – but they were both still adamant about directing. In the end, it probably came down to who had more muscle at the studio.

Warner Brothers paid us $500,000 in their purchase of *The Gauntlet* for Clint Eastwood.

There are words in the English language that come close to describing the depth and sweep of Clint's uncanny talent, but the words are long and rarely used, perhaps because not many people qualify. Clint Eastwood qualifies. He's a filmmaker's filmmaker.

Imagine this lanky kid from the San Fernando Valley with a limited education, becomes a bit player at Universal Studios in the '50s, gets cast in a supporting role in *Rawhide,* does three Westerns in Italy and goes on to build an unprecedented seven-decade career as one of the smartest actors, directors, and producers in the history of motion pictures. *Unforgiven, Mystic River, Million Dollar Baby*, and *Sully* are some of the best dramas of the past thirty years, and he's still making strong movies at the age of ninety-five. With all respect to both gentlemen, Clint Eastwood is three times the national treasure John Wayne was.

There was probably no bigger movie star in the 1970s, and Dennis and I were awed by what he did with *The Gauntlet*. He understood instinctively who Ben Shockley was and in casting Sondra Locke he provided Shockley with a perfect foil. He gave us a star turn in his scene with the biker gang, and in the verbal duel between Shockley, Mally and the Deputy, it was his savvy directorial restraint that gave the trio's confinement in that car the savage, witty, biting tension that made the scene sing.

He shot our script nearly verbatim, with only three notable differences: We'd originally had three hoboes in the boxcar and with masterly sleight-of-hand he replaced a hobo with one of the bikers; in an *homage* to his Dirty Harry persona he added Shockley's stoic, "Nag, nag, nag." Finally, it's possible that he added just a bit more gunfire to two of the movie's three fusillades than our screenplay had required – or so some folks believe. If it's true, it's totally consistent with the story's theme, and as a professor of film history at UCLA remarked long ago about such vivid movie moments, "*C'est du cinema!*" At any rate, there are no pyrotechnic excesses in the novel.

Speaking of the novel, now is probably an appropriate time for a transparency statement. Despite what the language on the cover asserts, neither Dennis nor I wrote the book. We never knew who did. Movie novelization writers are usually credited, and I have no idea why Warner Brothers and/or Malpaso Productions (Clint's company) chose not to identify this one. Whoever they may have been, it's clear that they worked from a combination of our finished script as well as some of Clint's changes prior to shooting – and an excellent job they did. I'm particularly impressed by the novelist's interpolation of Shockley's and Mally's unspoken inner life – their thoughts, their doubts, their pasts, particularly in two extended backstory flashbacks.

It's a smart, engaging read, and nearly half a century later I'm chuffed that Encyclopocalypse has reissued this rendition of our screenplay for a new audience.

It's probably fair to say that if *The Car* changed the course of our combined careers, *The Gauntlet* kicked us up to another level entirely.

Not long after *The Gauntlet*'s release, we wrote a *Dirty*

Harry script for Clint that didn't work for him. It was a crushing blow and we were devastated. We knew we'd never hear from him again. Orion Pictures loved the script, however, and bought it from Warner Brothers. Chuck Norris liked it too, and when the picture was released with Chuck starring, *Code of Silence* added a new demographic to his fan base and established director Andy Davis as a sought-after talent. We adapted George LaFountaine's novel *Flashpoint,* which became an excellent conspiracy thriller starring Kris Kristofferson and directed by Bill Tannen.

We wrote an action adventure called *Fifty/Fifty* about a bickering pair of mercenaries; it attracted Eddie Murphy and Sylvester Stallone for a week or so, and was finally produced more than a decade later with Peter Weller and Robert Hays (although Stallone may have been inspired by some of our concepts for *The Expendables*). We were hired to write a Mack Bolan/Executioner feature that never went anywhere. And we wrote a fun B-movie called *Bells,* which was eventually re-titled *Murder by Phone*. Then Dennis got a phone call in early 1978 and the unmistakeable voice on the other end had one simple question:

"Where's my Western?" asked Clint Eastwood.

We soon began writing what would become *Pale Rider*. But that's a story for another novelization…

Michael Butler
January 2026

PROLOGUE

"Be nice to him. Special nice..."

The words hovered above her like tracking gulls as she moved down the deserted hotel corridor. The plush blue carpet muffed her quick steps as she glanced left and right at ascending room numbers.

"He's a very special cop. We treat him right, he gives us the whole damn city of Phoenix."

It should have been a mindless routine, just like always.

But the admonition somehow made her intensely aware of her own movements—her long legs sweeping beneath the clinging dress, the fingers of her right hand gripping her evening bag a bit too tightly. Nervousness she didn't often feel; they didn't often give her such special instructions.

Then she was there, rapping briskly but softly on the door. A moment later it stood open. The man on the other side—broad and strong, dark-haired, wearing a black suit, the diagonal black and white stripes of his wide tie disappearing beneath a fully buttoned vest—nodded slightly, did not smile. She blinked and smiled at him. He stepped aside and let her enter.

Barely past him into the room, she heard the door close behind her, then the click of the lock snapping into place.

She didn't turn, walked on into the room. She felt strangely uneasy—before, because of what she had been told; now, because of him. Something.

Fool, she told herself. A man too uptight even to remove his coat? He's the nervous one. Except that he seemed so oddly calm, controlled.

She stepped to the nightstand by the double bed and set down her evening bag, took a breath, then turned to face him.

Her breath caught in her throat as she found him only inches away. He had moved so quickly.

She smiled, hoping it looked like a smile. He looked at her, not moving, not smiling. Forcing herself to gain control, she raised her arms and slid them around his big neck and drew herself up to him for a kiss. His lips were cold and unresponsive; his skin was like damp stone.

He kept his arms at his sides while she worked at his unyielding mouth. Then he reached one hand behind her and found the zipper at the back of her dress. He pulled it down with a smooth, unhurried movement.

She backed away, still smiling, hunched her shoulders forward, and let the lightweight fabric fall to the floor. She stepped out of her dress with accustomed nonchalance.

It would be better, now that things were in motion. She felt better. Confronting him in her black-mesh bra and panties, she twisted her smile seductively.

"Want to help me with the rest?"

"Finish it." Deep voice, cold like his mouth.

She shrugged and unhooked her bra, proud that her firm breasts actually needed no support, that the garment was merely titillating window dressing. Some liked it, some didn't.

No matter.

She kicked off her shoes in two quick motions. She wore

no stockings; her legs were firm and smooth and well-tanned.

She felt the deep, soft pile of the carpet on her feet.

She cocked her head and looked at him; he was looking at her hips. Slowly she hooked her thumbs under the elastic waistband of her panties, slid them languorously down over her hips and past the neat bulge of her crotch, and let them fall to the floor.

Confident in her nakedness, she stood before him, smiling coyly with half-closed eyes.

This moment was always hers, when they first saw her fully exposed, when her splendid body caused even the hardest among them to skip a breath. She stood eyeing him, letting her tongue flick out to moisten her lips, watching his face for the betrayal of his desire.

But his face showed nothing. Once again she felt a faint twinge of apprehension. There are all kinds, in this business.

She tilted her head back and put her hands on her round hips.

"How do you want it, lover?" Her tone lacked its usual edge of confidence now.

"Lie down. On your stomach." His voice, a growl from a pit.

Obediently, she turned away and went over to the bed and lay as directed, her view of the room then limited to a closed pair of blue draperies and a circular writing table flanked by two blue wicker chairs. She could not see the man.

She fought to keep the tenseness out of her body; her ears strained to hear him move.

Be nice to him...

Then he was in her view, standing by the writing table. Casually, he removed his suit coat and laid it carefully across one of the chairs.

Then he was gone, moving around to the foot of the bed.

But a vivid image lingered in her mind—a gun pressed close to the left side of his chest in a dull black shoulder holster.

Guns were common here, and he was a cop. Still…

She lay perfectly quiet, waiting. She would be nice to him.

"Open up."

Slowly she spread her legs, reminding herself that each passing second was bringing her that much closer to the moment when she'd be able to walk out the door.

The mattress sagged with his weight as he mounted the bed and worked his knees for position. She wanted to close her eyes, but she never did unless specifically asked. *You don't drop your guard in this business, baby.* She focused her eyes on his limp jacket draped across the chair, concentrated on it. Silence encased her like the pressure on a deep-sea diver.

She waited for the thrust.

Then it came. But it wasn't skin and muscle she felt enter her.

It was cold steel.

Her fists contracted, driving her carefully manicured fingernails hard into the palms of her hands as the gun barrel slid deeper into her body.

She dared not speak, or make any sound at all, or move.

She must lie and wait and make him welcome. Her senses were agonizingly acute to each nuance of his activity. And so she heard it—the light rasp of his zipper being undone; and then she sensed the pulsating rhythmic pumping of his hand on his own flesh.

Then his voice, the throaty gravel of his words chilling her like a graveyard fog.

"Scream and I'll pull the trigger."

She felt rare tears form in her eyes, felt her teeth bite sharply into her lower lip. Above it all his words echoed in her mind, the ungodly threat mingling with her own desperate prayer for him to finish with her.

Be nice to him...

She was being nice.

CHAPTER 1

The unseasonal heat shimmered over the city, turning what should have been a pleasant, early-morning balm into an oppressive harbinger of another stifling day. It had been hot for a week.

Detective Ben Shockley was on his second cup of black coffee, his eyes roaming listlessly over the marble-patterned plastic that covered the two-place breakfast bar in his apartment. Only partially listening to the news broadcast that droned from a portable radio at his elbow, he became gradually aware of a weatherman launching into a cheerful explanation of upper-level lows.

"Shit," Ben said to the babbling voice, "it's gonna be hot. Period." He clicked it off.

He wanted another cup of coffee. But he was already jittery. And it would make him hotter. He was a morning person, and ordinarily it was easy to get going. Moods for him came later in the day, when he got fed up with the routine. But this morning he was black, cranky, angry before he'd even talked to another human being.

He wasn't pleased with the way he was acting, but then he wasn't pleased with what had happened yesterday, either.

Yesterdays were for forgetting, which, with years of practice, he was usually able to do. You couldn't let one day's garbage drift over into the next in this business; you'd be covered with it in a week. Because every day was filled with it. Cops who couldn't ditch it after every tour became maniacs and took it out either on the garbage or on themselves. Ben Shockley started every day clean of yesterday's garbage.

But not this one. He'd gone over it in his mind time and again during the past twenty-four hours. He'dd gone to sleep thinking about it and woke up the same.

Why Josie?

That was the question he'd been asking himself since ten o'clock yesterday morning. But what he really meant was: Why not me?

Shockley and Meynard Josephson had, in police jargon, been "on the bricks" together for fifteen years. They'd been uniformed patrolmen together, then plainclothes, then detectives. They'd trusted each other with their lives on countless occasions—countless because you *couldn't* count them; cops never knew when their lives were on the line, or when they weren't. The average John Q Public figured that when guns didn't come out, nobody was in danger. Fuck John Q.

What he knew was that he and Josie had trusted each other with their lives, protected each other, come to know each other's moves and subtle signals—which is the stuff good teams are made of. And their working partnership had slowly evolved into the strong bond of friendship.

Friendship: too weak a word. They were a unit. Good cops have to be friends; they couldn't be friends with anybody else. What the hell could you talk to a John Q about?

John Q looked down his nose at the people who kept their city safe for democracy and profit. People like Ben Shockley and Josie. They were good cops, both proud of their detective's shields. And Shockley was convinced that if their records were compared point for point, reprimand for reprimand, citation for citation, there would be no significant difference.

That, of course, might have been the reason behind the whole thing. Their similarity of performance may have rendered the entire selection process a coin-toss operation. After all, a sudden vacancy had to be filled. There was a promotion to be made. And how would *he* have chosen between the two of them if their records had been tossed on his desk for a decision?

Josie was a family man; Shockley was not. All else being equal, give the family man the desk, leave the other poor bastard out there to take the heat. Why not? Nobody wants a weeping kid at a funeral. Too goddam dramatic. He hadn't even fired his gun since... never shot anybody, anyway. And never been seriously shot at, not hit. More firemen buy the farm than cops.

Jesus! Shockley shook his head. What a foul goddam mood. He swallowed the last of his coffee and set the mug down with a sharp rap on the counter. He was damn jealous, and he didn't like the way it felt; didn't like the schoolboy nature of it.

What was that phrase the police psychologist was always using in those "reorientation" sessions? "Getting in touch with your feelings," that was it. Well, he was in touch with them, all right, and he'd come to the conclusion that he'd have been a hell of a lot better off if he and his feeling had remained total strangers.

Didn't that goddam shrink understand cops? Feelings are risky, make you crazy. Shrinks don't know shit from Shinola about cops.

Without taking his feelings to bed with him, he could have bought himself off with five or six bourbons and a twenty-five dollar lay and that would have been the end of it.

Hey, Josie—he would have liked to say—fuck your pro motion, let's get a buzz on and our rocks off.

Josie was a family man. Shockley would have had to drink alone. A bad idea for even John Q; disaster for a cop.

He knew he was acting like a juvenile bastard, and the knowledge of it only served to blacken his already ebony mood.

Glancing out of the window at the unyielding brightness of the morning, he carried his coffee mug over to the sink and gave it a token squirt of water. He rarely dirtied dishes, more rarely washed them. He preferred the quick-food convenience of a cheeseburger and fries at a greasy spoon-where he could walk away from his garbage, rather than make a mess at home, which served to remind him that he was so single.

Also, he was onto the fact that he was a singularly lousy cook. Instant coffee was enough of a bore.

He left the cramped kitchen and stalked out to the main living area, a small rectangle that opened onto a narrow balcony. These rooms, together with a bathroom/shower, comprised what was euphemistically referred to in the real estate trade as a "bachelor apartment."

Like his dress and habits, his surroundings were austere: leatherette sofa-bed, two spindly-legged chairs, a three-light, brass-finish pole lamp, and a dull, stained slab of a coffee table. There were no pictures on the stark white walls, no mementoes proudly displayed. All in all, a barren reflection of a barren life, a spartan depot for his comings and goings.

But it served him well, was his view of it, and he'd long since rid himself of the illusion that he needed anything more. Or that anything more would help.

With a practiced movement that he took as much for granted as opening a door or tuning a car key, he collapsed the sofa-bed on itself and tossed the cushions into place. Then he slipped on the jacket of his eight-year-old worsted, reminding himself again that he had to send the damn thing out to be pressed, patted his pockets to make sure his keys and wallet were in place, and his waist for the gun, and left.

The drive to the precinct was such a well-established routine that he often thought he could do it in his sleep. And there certainly had been more than one occasion when the extended drudgery of an investigation had nearly forced a test of his theory.

This morning, however, his mind was fully occupied with the nagging knowledge that today he'd be drawing his new partner. He'd been mentally reviewing a list of possibilities once the reality of Josie's promotion had settled into him.

There were some good ones and some not so good, some he'd rather not risk even sitting in a car with. And of course it might be someone he'd never met or heard of before.

But whatever the selection, his adjustment to the new man wouldn't be easy; that much he was sure of. Would his new partner be so apprehensive? Shit, no; the new man would be younger, in all probability, and thrilled to death to be teamed with a veteran.

Old Josie. You didn't separate yourself from fifteen years with a shrug of the shoulders and a firm handshake. After that much time together, there was a hell of a lot more to it, and Shockley viewed the prospect with anything but optimism. He swung his Riviera into the parking lot, parked and locked it. He'd have to remember to get it washed.

He entered the station by the rear door and was in the midst of his usual hellos when Detective Lieutenant Bronson approached him in the squad room.

"Hey, Ben, see you a minute?"

"Hey, Ted." He followed the lieutenant over to a desk. "What's up?"

"You got an appointment."

"Yeah, I know. I draw a new partner today."

"Later. Right now this takes precedence. Blakelock wants to see you."

•Why?"

"Internal Affairs doesn't have to give a reason."

"Or even have one," Shockley muttered.

"Come on..."

"That stinks, Ted. Internal Affairs calls for me, I want to know what's going down."

"Hey, I just work here, remember? I haven't heard of any trouble regarding you. All I know is, the man said to send you over as soon as you came in. So consider yourself sent."

"Thanks a hell of a lot."

Bronson smiled. "The quicker you get your ass over there, the quicker you'll find out what it's all about, and the quicker you can tell us all about it."

"Yeah," Shockley said sullenly. "If he calls back, tell him me and my ass are on our way. Let's hope neither one comes back in a sling."

"Shockley?" The sergeant bellowed the name into the crowded waiting room, causing Ben to wince. Being called in by Internal Affairs—the outfit that investigates cops within the department—was bad enough without your name bounced off the walls.

Ben rose casually from his chair.

"Lieutenant Commander Blakelock will see you now."

Shockley crossed the room with his usual slow, steady gait.

He hurried for no one—you learned not to jump, on the street. And though he was curious about his summons by Internal Affairs, he certainly wasn't scared. He was clean as anybody in the department—cleaner, maybe. And if he was being called in to rat on some other officer—well, he didn't know anything worth knowing. Believe it or not.

Anyway, he had too much respect for fear to waste it on office confrontations.

The sergeant twisted a doorknob and shoved the door open. Ben walked through and stared across a broad desk at the Lieutenant Commander.

A man in his early fifties who either dyed his black hair or kept it otherwise weeded of gray, wearing a three-piece suit that put Shockley's tired worsted to shame, Blakelock radiated an aura of unimpeachable, humorless authority. Probably safe and steady enough, but not a man that Shockley would care to share a squad car with.

The commander openly studied the detective, expressionlessly, as if measuring him for—well, a suit.

Then, blinking quickly as if waking up, he spoke. "I'm Blakelock."

Shockley blinked, too, at the sound of his voice—the startling basso of a man whose larynx had been tampered with.

"Shockley," he said.

"Sit down if you like."

"No, thank you, sir." He tried a smile. "I'll be on my rump most of the day." He wished immediately he hadn't said it, to a man who probably always sat.

Blakelock was undisturbed. "Ever served with us before... unh... Shockley?"

"Served? No sir. Never even been into Internal before."

Blakelock tapped the edge of an envelope against the palm of his hand and pondered Shockley's belt buckle. "We... Internal Affairs... have a considerable responsibility... I'm sure you know..." He glanced up. "Watchdog of the department... policing the police. The need for... absolute security... is imperative. Is that clear?"

Shockley shuffled his feet. "Yessir, I understand. that What I don't understand is why I'm here."

Blakelock leaned back in his swivel chair and blinked, as if caught by surprise in his monologue.

Shockley cleared his throat, in sympathy for Blakelock's own tortured mechanism.

Blakelock narrowed his eyes and peered at Shockley's face.

"You're not in trouble, Detective Shockley." Inexplicably, he smiled.

"Thank you, sir."

The commander suddenly leaned forward and thrust the envelope he was holding across the desk toward Shockley.

Hesitantly, Shockley picked it up, but didn't open it.

The commander nodded at the envelope. "Those are plane tickets… extradition subpoena. You're flying to Las Vegas… bringing back a prisoner for us, whom you will remand to custody at… unh… County. Then you'll report back here. To no one else but me. Understand?"

"Respectfully, sir, I work for Metro Squad. Why me?"

Blakelock stared at him with a face as stony as a cinder block wall.

"Our personnel is… occupied. Your division commander says you're a man who gets the job done."

"So are a lot of others."

Blakelock leaned forward over the desk, rubbing his hands together. "But I picked you."

"Yessir, sorry." He *was* sorry. He was a cooperative cop. "Is there, unh, anything I should know about the case?"

"What it is," Blakelock rasped, "is this: a nothing witness for a nothing trial… Just has to be done."

Shockley nodded and looked at the envelope. A garbage assignment. First he'd lost out on a promotion, now he was an errand boy for Internal Affairs.

"That'll be all, Detective," Blakelock growled as he re turned to the paperwork on his desk.

"Yessir." *Fuck you, Lieutenant Commander, sir.* But he nodded politely, turned, and let himself out.

"There's no justice in the world," Josie muttered, his protruding belly crowding the steering wheel as he guided the car through the last wave of morning traffic. "We spend fifteen years together, and look what happens. I draw a lousy desk job, and you get a freebie to Vegas."

*Yeah," Stockley grunted, "my big break. A two-bit witness for a two-bit trial. They probably sat up all night trying to pick the right guy for the assignment."

"Don't knock it. At least it's a ticket out of this goddam heat." He swerved to avoid a halted taxi. "What's it all about, Ben?

"Haven't the foggiest."

"Hey," Josie turned to him, "you ain't holding out on me?"

"No, goddam it, no!" In fifteen years Josie hadn't suggested such a thing, and Shockley had never held out. "That's all I know. Internal wouldn't trust me with fact one about it."

"Weird."

"What the hell's weird about it?" Shockley gritted his teeth. So quickly this tiny wedge between them. "They're always weird, up there."

"Yeah. Least you ain't in trouble."

"Yeah." He glanced across at his friend. Even Josie's roughhewn face—a face he used to joke was put together out of spare parts—couldn't hide the trace of tension that existed between the two men. They'd become such an efficient, well-oiled unit over the years that neither had ever entertained any serious thoughts about one outstripping the other within the department. Yet it had happened. He hoped they could ride it out and stay close.

In any event, Ben had to admit he was thankful for the

release from his daily routine. Maybe that was even the reason for his drawing the assignment. Though he knew he was probably reading a great deal into a simple coincidence.

He was anxious to get on the plane and get the job done.

Josie tapped the steering wheel and hummed a few notes.

"So, at least you must know the name of the witness."

"Yeah."

"Anybody I know?"

Shockley pulled the envelope from his inside jacket pocket and took the extradition papers out of it. He scanned the document, finally tracing his finger under the name. "Gus Mally. Ever heard of him?"

"Don't ring a bell. But anybody could be using that name. Could even be something Internal Affairs stuck on him, for cover. God bless the headhunters, Ben. They do love their games, don't they?"

"You ever meet Blakelock?"

"No, but I've heard enough about him. He runs his division like a goddam sovereign territory.

"Powerful man."

"*Too* powerful, for my money. Like a goddam invisible octopus. You never know whether you're on a real case, or whether you're being set up to see if you can be bought—and wrecked. He's got authority he hasn't even used yet."

"*Somebody* has to have it," Shockley said. "Crooked cops can get you iced, to say nothing of what they make John Q think of all of us. Somebody's gotta weed out the rotten..."

Josie was laughing, then Ben, too. The lines were like right out of department public relations. The fact was, nobody liked Internal Affairs, because they were always looking over your shoulder, and if they thought you'd done something wrong, they could break you. To straight cops like Ben and Josie, they were a necessary evil. But they didn't help morale, with their snooping and suspicions; and morale was hard enough to keep up in this business, dealing with scum all the time, then being spat on for it by John Q, who saw all cops as dumb sadists.

"What's he like, old Blakelock?" Josie asked.

"I wouldn't want him on my tail."

"Tough, huh?"

"I don't think he'd give a shit what he did to get you, if he was after you. He's not what you'd call a laugh-a-minute."

"Well, he ain't after you."

"Nope."

"And at least he can send you to Vegas if he wants. Can't argue with that."

Shockley refolded the documents and stuffed them back in his coat pocket. "Look, I'm going there, turning around, and coming right back. You wouldn't even have time to get laid."

"You wouldn't have time." Josie grinned, glad to be back on more familiar ground with his friend. "Still getting serviced by that Shirley broad?"

"Not any more."

"Why the hell not? She had a great ass."

"Good. Not great."

"Okay, so we got different standards. Why'd you let her go?"

"Straight story?"

"Hell, yes?

"I found out she was after me for my money."

Josie guffawed and almost missed the turn into the airport parking garage.

"Jesus, it must be damn near eighty already." Tiny beads of perspiration stood out on Josie's wide face as the two men walked briskly toward the terminal.

"Maybe you'll sweat off a couple of pounds."

"Not with the lunch Helen packed for me."

"You telling me you're gonna brown-bag it your first day at your desk?"

Josie flashed a sheepish grin. "We had roast pork for dinner last night. You know what a sucker I am for a cold pork sandwich."

"Along with anything else."

"Shit, guy like you has all the luck. Metabolism keeps you lean. And what the hell. I'm married, Ben. I gotta have *some* vices."

"Then pick a healthy one, for chrissake." Two pneumatic doors swung open in front of them. "Gonna be worse, with you sitting behind a desk all day."

"You always been thin. Maybe if you got married, you'd be fat."

"Who needs it?"

"Yeah. Sometimes I feel like I been married forever, you know what I mean? I could envy you, sometimes."

Ben chuckled. Josie was a happily married man; he said things like that once in a while just to make Ben feel better.

They stepped inside and were struck by a cold wall of air-conditioning. Josie stopped to breathe in the chilly relief and blot his forehead and cheeks with a rumpled handkerchief.

"Now, that's more like it."

"Terrific," Ben said. "You'll probably get pneumonia."

"Not me. Germs got too much fat to go through."

"Germs love fat. They go right after fat, married, desk men first of all."

Shockley confirmed the departure time on an overhead television monitor, and they walked to the gate. People were already checking in. Josie hooked a thumb in the direction of the giant aircraft looming on the opposite side of the glass wall.

"Christ almighty," he whistled, "it looks like the Queen Mary with wings. You ever been on one like that before?"

"Nope."

"Shit. Something that big must have eight stews roaming the aisles. You lucky bastard."

"So I get to sit and look. You've been reading too many paperbacks, Josie. I'm going and I'm coming, that's all there is to it."

"Yeah, yeah, I know. Hey, why don't you give me a buzz at the precinct and I'll shoot over and pick you up? Then after we drop off the garbage you can come over for dinner."

"Not tonight. I could get held up. But say hello to Helen and the kids for me. And thanks for the lift. I know how busy you executives are."

"In your ear."

"Whatever gets you off. And in case I never said it before," Ben glanced shyly at him, "congratulations on the promotion."

Josie shifted his feet awkwardly and stared at the floor.

"Shit," he said softly, "I don't know why they picked me.

You and me were partners, for crissake. They didn't have to split—"

"They picked you because you deserved it."

Both men looked away.

"But I hate paperwork, you know that. If it wasn't for the family, I'd tell "em to take their desk job and shove it."

Ben clapped him on the back. "Quit bellyaching. You're off the bricks. Enjoy it."

The hollow tones of a female voice on the public address system interrupted to announce the flight.

"Catch you later," Shockley said as he moved toward the line of people at the gate.

"Hey!"

Ben stopped and turned back.

A lopsided grin spread across Josie's spare-parts face. "We went through a lot of doors together, Ben. Damn, we had our times."

Shockley paused for a moment, an uncomfortable

mixture of contradictory feelings roiling in him. He winked at Josie.

"We had our times, all right."

The two men waved, turned, and moved off in opposite directions.

Once Ben had disappeared through the gate, Josie turned back and looked through the glass at the plane. He didn't in fact know if he wanted the desk job. Things were right away different between him and Ben. He felt somehow naked, unprotected, with Ben leaving on an assignment divorced from their partnership.

The truth was, things had been different for a while. At first, when Josie got married, they had made it a threesome for dinners or movies or parties; a foursome when Ben had a date. But then when the kids came, well, it changed. Josie spent more time at home, and got involved with his kids, and he and Ben had less to talk about.

But their closeness went far deeper.

They didn't have to talk about Josie's kids; they were partner cops, depending on each other.

In fact, Ben had made Josie the cop he was. Ben was such a standup guy, dependable, conscientious without being dull.

They shared their cases like tag-team wrestlers, one always right there to take the lead when the other was in trouble or tired—except that there was nothing fake about it. The people they went up against weren't always dangerous, but sometimes they were, and you never knew which it was.

There was no script. What was always the same, the rock both clung to, was that they were equal partners, each always ready to go the route for the other.

And Ben was such a goddam smart cop—not ambitious, but smart. And dogged. When they were on a case, the case was going to be solved, wrapped up neatly and tied with a bow. Big or small, they'd wrap it up. And the credit was shared, collar for collar.

More often than not, it was Ben's brains that actually solved the case. He would charge full speed ahead into a situation, once he had it knocked. And it was Josie's normal role to back him up. Josie was the more cautious one, more watchful of surrounding danger, more intent on protecting Ben and getting him out of holes alive.

Like when Ben rousted that gunrunner in that abandoned building, and left the guy's sweet-looking old lady alone behind him, and she quietly pulled heat out of her purse and leveled it at the back of Ben's ear, it was Josie who was ready for it, who smacked her gun hand away.

Josie watched the plane taxi off. *Ben should be at the desk,* he thought. H*e should be running the whole damn detective bureau.* If only he could get Ben to care a little about his whole damn future. And lately he'd been hitting the sauce a bit heavy, Josie knew.

The massive plane hurtled down the runway, the vibration filtering through Shockley's body like a welcomed massage. Then suddenly it ceased, and as he looked out of his small rectangle of window the earth dropped away beneath him in a diminishing landscape of rooftops and pencil-thin highways, the dots of cars like so many frantic, scurrying ants.

The two seats next to him were empty. Shockley reached for a copy of the airline's magazine in the seat-back pocket in front of him. He thumbed through the glossy, colorful pages of travel and adventure that seemed to mock his dreary assignment.

"Care for a cocktail, sir?"

The attractive stewardess—slender, with honey-blonde hair, vivid blue eyes, and the chic, well-scrubbed look standard for her work—smiled down at him.

Shockley caught himself staring. “Can you do a Bloody Mary?”

“Surely. It'll be just a few minutes.”

She moved down the aisle collecting other drink orders.

Her hips were round and a treat to watch—he'd have to remember to tell Josie.

Soon his drink arrived on a small tray, the seasoned tomato juice in a plastic glass and a miniature bottle of vodka next to it.

“A dollar fifty, please.”

Shockley dug the money from his pocket. She thanked him and moved on. Ben wondered what she really felt behind her easy smile and bright blue eyes. It was the way he sized up anybody, in his work. He decided that she was thinking about what obscene but accurate nickname she would secretly assign to each of the lecherous men in her section—which was all of them.

Including, he thought with a touch of embarrassment, himself. It had been a while since…

He sampled his drink. Not bad. His usual drink was bourbon, but he'd opted for the Mary in recognition of the hour.

Been on the stuff quite a bit lately, which probably had something to do, he had to admit, with his morning moods recently. Ordinarily he didn't drink on duty, but this was not what he considered duty. Not for a fifteen-year veteran, and a detective.

He wasn't drinking for pleasure, but to take the edge off his feelings about Josie's promotion and the inertia of his own career—his own life, for that matter.

Not that he took his assignment lightly; it was his job, and he would do it—fast, professionally, and with no questions asked. Except that this time he had questions. For example, what was this all about? He was a detective, for chrissake, not a damn rookie kid patrolman, and he had a right to know.

He drained his glass and looked out of the window at the

fleecy tapestry of brilliant white clouds. Once, so many years ago, when he'd flown to his father's funeral, the clouds had looked the same way—a cotton candy landscape daring him to step from the plane and walk among the fluffy hills and gossamer valleys. The clouds were an illusion of substance, once a comforting beauty, now a symbol of his distrust of beauty. Nice things, gentle things, beautiful things could not bear the weight of reality.

His old man had been a gentle person, patient, quiet. The old man was sad, too, Ben pieced together much later, because nobody in Chicago wanted to hire a fine cabinet maker anymore. The last thing Ben remembered him saying was, "Better to be a cop, at least it's secure." The closest the old man came to being a cop was to buy an old pistol. He'd put the old pistol to his head. The funeral was in Sioux City, which was where they had come from, and where the paid-up plot was.

And so Ben had ultimately become a cop, though not by a direct route, and not because of anything he consciously connected to his father. He didn't know what, if anything, he felt about the old man; feelings were garbage you put aside.

You put them aside by not caring and not having anybody to care about. It had been that way for him. Except, of course, for that brief time with Judy, who finally decided that being a cop's wife was entirely too insecure.

The irony in that didn't occur to Ben, just the loss. Now the cops had taken Josie away from him. No big deal. Just that he could trust Josie with his life.

Well, he could survive without Josie, for chrissake. His work had become so goddam routine that there was precious little risk left. And now this fucking, pointless trip.

Far below stretched the flat, parched, interminable desert.

Fitting, he thought. An arid no-man's land, and he was being sent into it to drag out a hapless witness to an unknown crime—or maybe not even a crime, maybe just some violation of departmental regulations that would cost some poor bastard his badge. Who knows about Internal Affairs?

He pushed the call button to order another drink, got it, and found himself cold even to the brush of the stewardess's fine hip on his arm. He loosened his tie, laid his head back, and closed his eyes.

There was just no reason why he should be on his way to Vegas, and that was all there was to it. He should be back on the bricks, with Josie. That's where they both belonged.

Neither of them was good at anything else. What the hell, didn't the goddam paper-jockeys know enough not to pull a guy's partner on him after fifteen years?

He opened his eyes and looked out. Just desert. No serenity there, only loneliness and desolation bisected by a thin ribbon of highway uniting nowhere with infinity.

Josie can't even spell, *for chrissake!*

He raised his glass to his lips and proposed a silent toast.

To Gus Mally. Whoever the hell you are.

CHAPTER 2

Shockley made his way quickly through the terminal at McCarran International, past the clusters of strategically placed slot machines, and out to the waiting row of taxi cabs.

A driver intercepted him as he approached the lead cab. "Got any luggage?"

"Nothing," Ben said. "Just get me to the police station."

"You got it, pal."

Ben slid into the back seat, and the cab swept into the flow of airport traffic. He had an innate dislike for public vehicles, and this one smelled of stale cigar smoke and cheap perfume, the former being traceable to the balding, beer-bellied driver.

"You a lawyer or something?" The cabbie spoke between teeth clamped on a soggy cigar.

"Yeah, something." It was a reflex of some unknown root, not to say he was a cop.

"Gonna be in town long?"

"I'll be out on the first flight I can get."

"Too bad. Action's good this time of year."

"Glad to hear it."

"Fella like you, look like you could use some action. I could give you a line on—"

"Only action I need is what it takes to get me to the P.D. How much farther is it?"

"Not long. Relax and enjoy the view. Sure you don't—"

"Drop it."

The cabbie shrugged and puffed out a blue plume of smoke. They turned onto Las Vegas Boulevard, "The Strip," and the view even in broad daylight, was an archetype of gaudy splendor. The combination of tinted glass towers, Roman statuary, graceful fountains, and mammoth marquees melded into a pulsating advertisement for all the pleasures to which the human condition is heir.

But to Ben, the hammer-blow bombardment that surrounded him amounted to nothing more than a neon-and-concrete bore.

The Las Vegas police station was a stark affair, but Shockley was glad to be rid of the foul-smelling cab and its talkative driver.

He paid his fare, left a less than generous tip, and waited for the inevitable smart remark. But the cabbie's only reaction was to bite harder on his cigar stump and drive away.

Ben was grateful for that small favor; the department hassled you on reimbursements for tipping, as if giving cops taxi rides should be a public service.

Wouldn't it be sweet, Ben thought, to come to Vegas with time *and* money? Win something, lose something, stay all night with a whore (something he'd never done), start all over the next day, leave whenever you damn felt like it, go back to your executive's desk high up in some fancy building, and count your money until you could come again.

Some cops were able to do that somehow. That's why you had people like Blakelock and outfits like Internal Affairs.

Inside the station, the clatter of typewriters and the underlying hum of police-argot conversation greeted Ben with the eerie feeling that he'd never left his precinct. All P.D.'s were the same; no amount of architectural finesse could alter the unique brand of business that was carried on within their walls, or the sloppy clutter of papers and paraphernalia that resulted from it. Cops were a mess because their business was messy, and because John Q figured they could operate on a piss-ant budget because cops were so happy kicking people around they'd do it for nothing.

Casually, Shockley approached the desk sergeant. The gray-haired veteran glanced up, then looked back down at his paperwork. "What can I do for you?"

Ben produced his detective's shield and rapped it on the desk to get the man's attention. "Name's Ben Shockley, Phoenix P.D. I got an extradite for a prisoner. Mally. Gus Mally."

"See Sergeant Grady." A hand waved to the left. "Through there. How's the weather down your way?"

"Hot. Thanks." Shockley slipped his shield back in his coat pocket and walked through the squad room toward a green door standing ajar.

He rapped once and walked in. Sergeant Grady was a stubbly man—two piggish eyes and an alcohol-pickled nose; a body designed to sit behind a desk, perhaps never to move from it. Ben imagined him attached with suitable plumbing to the floor.

Grady looked up lethargically when Ben entered. "Yeah?" The word oozed out between fat lips.

Ben flashed his shield again. "Shockley, Phoenix P.D. Here to pick up a prisoner, guy named Mally. Maybe you got a Telex on it."

Grady listened without expression, then leaned back in his chair. The movement was accompanied by an agonizing groan of springs. No plumbing; he was a free man. "Man named Mally, you say?"

"That's right." Ben put his shield away. "Gus Mally."

"Well," Grady groaned with the springs, "let's have a look and see what we've got." He thrust a puffy hand into a desk drawer and pulled out a dingy file folder, used over and over again by the looks of the crossed-out scribblings on it. With great care and deliberation, as if launching a momentous task, he opened the file, pulled out sheets of paper, and began scanning them. At last he looked up at Ben, raising his eyebrows in innocent surprise. "Your man's not here."

"What?" Ben blinked. "What do you mean he's not here?"

"Just what I said, bud." Grady shrugged and looked back at the papers.

Ben yanked the extradition documents from his coat pocket and shoved them under the sergeant's twitching nose.

"This is a subpoena for one Gus Mally. This is the address of this jail. Now check again. If you please."

Grady, outranked but with the home-turf advantage, sighed and picked up the file again. He traced his finger under the names one at a time, commenting pleasantly: "Got me lots of fellas here. Got me a Fisher... a Burger... a Sprague... a Adelman... a Terwilliger... a Gonzales... Take your pick. Take 'em all, far's I care. But I ain't got me no fella named Mally—not in *this* jail."

Shockley snapped the booking sheet from his hands and quickly scanned the list of prisoners' names, his anger rising as he reached the end of the page with no mention of Mally.

"Damn!" He slapped the list down. "He was supposed to have been arrested last night and held here for extradition. Shit." He paced back and forth. "Somebody screwed up."

Grady smiled. "Kinda looks that way, don't it?"

"Shit." Ben turned and headed for the door.

"Remember, now," Grady piped after him, "when you get back home empty-handed, all I said was I ain't got no *guy* named Gus Mally."

Ben stopped in mid-stride and spun back at the sergeant,

who now wore a closed-lip grin that arced up around the corners of his nose.

"*Augustina* Mally, I got." Grady waggled a finger victoriously. "Right here—in women's detention."

CHAPTER 3

Shockley stood in the cell, a gray, dank square with a sink and a commode on adjoining corner walls. A chunky prison matron in a pale blue uniform stood next to him. Their eyes focused on a shapeless lump huddled beneath a blanket on the cot along one wall.

"She's been spitting up since morning," the matron said.

"Looks like she's got a fever or something. I called the prison doctor, but he didn't show. Ain't that the way? Just like if a prisoner's sick it don't matter none, even though they get paid for—"

"Okay, Mally, hit the deck!" Ben's voice bounced off the cold cell walls, causing the matron to jump. But there was no response from the motionless form under the blanket. Ben sighed and turned to the matron. "She eat anything at all?"

"Just a cup of coffee this morning. That's all she wanted, just coffee."

Ben gave a quick glance around, walked to the sink, and picked up an empty coffee mug. He peered into it, passed it back and forth under his nose, then gave an almost imperceptible nod of satisfaction.

"Find something?" the matron asked.

"Yeah. She smoked a couple of butts and mixed the ashes

in with the brew. Old army trick. She *wanted* to look sick. And that'll do it, every time."

"Well, don't that beat…" The matron took the mug from him and copied his movements, passing it under her nose.

Suddenly the blanket flew into the air as Gus Mally erupted from the cot and dove for the half-open cell door. Ben sprang, grabbed her by the rear of her faded gray prison dress, and dragged her, kicking and screaming, back into the cell, where he pacified her quickly with a resounding slap across the face that caused the matron to jump again.

Ben pinned Mally's arms against the wall, and they had their first close-up look at each other.

Though no classical beauty, Augustina Mally possessed a strong, sensual quality that held Ben's eyes. In her thirties, she had a firm and rounded body that looked ten years younger. Her hair was blonde and long. Her mouth was lush, marred only by a faint scar at the left corner. Her eyes flashed with street wisdom and an iron will. She was stronger than she looked—either that or she was more intent on breaking free than Ben would have expected, given the hopelessness of her circumstances.

For her part, what Mally saw was a tall, lean, dark-haired man in his mid-forties wearing a rumpled suit and staring at her impassively with dark, lazy eyes. He, too, was stronger than he looked.

The corners of Mally's mouth curled with contempt.

"Terrific," she snarled. "My life's on the line, and they send me an on-the-ropes bum."

"I'm a detective, Mally," he said, matter-of-factly, "and I've got an extradition order for you."

"I could smell cop before you even came in here."

Ben turned to the matron. "She have a record?"

"Hooker."

He looked back at Mally, his arms still pinioning her against the wall. He spoke with a weary monotone born of too many years of hookers and narcs and winos. "Look, we've got a problem, you and me. We don't like each other much, but we've got to take a trip together. Now, you can come peaceably, or you can be a pain in the ass. You decide. But if you mess around, I'll put the bracelets on; if you talk dirty, I'll gag you; if you try to run, I'll shoot you. My name's Shockley, and we've got a plane to catch. So let's go."

Without waiting for an answer, he moved away from the wall, dropping Mally's arms.

"Wait." The matron stepped to the cell door and barred it with her brawny arms.

"What's the matter?" Ben asked.

"They're still cutting her papers."

"What! That shoulda been done hours ago. What the hell kind of a lock-up is this?"

"It's not my fault. They knew you were coming, all right. I don't know why they didn't do it earlier."

"Okay okay." He glanced back at Mally who stood rubbing her wrists where Ben had held them. "Just tell them to hurry their ass, will you?"

The matron waddled out of the cell, swinging the barred door shut behind her.

"So." Ben crossed his arms and peered at Mally. "What's it gonna be?"

She leaned hard against the wall, pressing her palms on the stone beside her hips. "You got a super way with women."

He made no response.

"But you're in over your head this time, cop."

"Don't let it get out."

"Shit." She turned toward the wall and clenched her fists.

"Right now I'm going to get some lunch. While I'm gone, think about that little speech I made."

"You mean the one about all the nasty things the big strong policeman is going to do to me if I misbehave? Don't worry, I believed every marvelous word of it. You're very convincing."

"Good. Just so we understand each other." He started toward the cell door.

"You'll never get me back to Phoenix, mister."

He leaned his face between the bars and looked out.

"Because you're a dead man, Shockley."

Something in the calmness of the remark made him turn around. He cocked his head.

"They're going to kill me," Mally said firmly. "If you're with me, they'll kill you, too."

"Sure they will." He arched his eyebrows. "Who's 'they'?"

She hesitated a moment, then spoke quietly. "I don't know."

"Okay. Then why are 'they' after you?"

"I don't know that, either."

"But they're going to kill you."

"Yes."

"Well, then," he said, "it's lucky there's a cop around, when you need one."

She glared at him, unblinking. "For you," she said evenly, "I don't give a shit. But you take me out of here, I'm dead."

He nodded and smiled slightly. "Pack your lipstick, Mally."

He turned and pounded on the door for the warder.

"Dammit!" she snapped, taking a step toward him. "It's the truth! They've even got a *line* on it. On *us!*"

"Line?"

"Betting line, dimwit! Odds!"

Ben chuckled. "They bet on a lot of things here. Ponies. Football. The fights. Any kind of action at all. But nobody gives a damn about a lard-ass cop holding hands with a two-bit hooker on an airplane." He hammered again for the warder.

Mally bit her lip. She softened her voice, but spoke with

even more urgency. "Shockley, will you listen to me? It's fifty-to-one we don't make it. The grapevine's good in here. Fifty-to-one. If you don't believe me, ask any bookie."

"First one I see."

She stepped quickly up to him and stood leaning against the cell door with folded arms, peering at his face. She heard the approaching footsteps of the warder and the clink of keys. "Christ!" She spun away and stalked to the rear of the cell. "Christ almighty!" Her voice quavered. "Is it so hard to check with a goddam bookie? Huh? What the hell have you got to lose?"

"Time. This goddam place has already held me up."

The cell door was opened for him, and he stepped outside.

The door swung shut; the warder twisted the key in the lock and walked away.

Mally sprang to the door, gripping the bars and thrusting her face harshly into them. "Listen, listen to me!" she whispered plaintively. "Don't be deaf, dumb, *and* blind!"

He started off down the corridor.

"Time," she hissed, "you'll take time for lunch, but not the time to find out if there's somebody out there waiting to blow you away."

He turned and looked at her. "Don't drown yourself in the sink." He walked off, hearing her thud back onto the cot.

CHAPTER 4

He'd meant to have lunch, but eating alone was a drag, and the hassles at the jail had taken away his appetite. So he sat in the bar, nursing his second bourbon. He told himself he wasn't on duty, just waiting to *go* on duty, once the paperwork was done and he could take his prisoner. He'd cut back some other day, some easier day.

The waitress edged over. A chesty, fortyish woman with dirty brown hair lacquered to a brittle beehive, she slid the bourbon bottle along the bar toward him. "Freshen it for you, mister?"

"No thanks." He wiped his mouth with a paper napkin that had a dirty cartoon on it.

"Maybe some pretzels?" She slid the brown plastic bowl toward him.

"Just the check. I got a plane to catch."

She took the bill out of her apron pocket, did some quick figuring on it, and shoved it in front of him. "Pay me up front, at the register."

"Fine. In a minute."

"You know," she leaned over the bar, her folded arms pushing her big breasts up, "there's no way you'd get me in a plane. No, sir. Not after all the pilots I've dated. I wouldn't let those guys drive my *car.*" She leaned back and nodded sharply once.

"Yeah," Ben said, tilting his glass for the final swig.

"Just last week," she leaned across the bar again, her voice confidential, "I was just reading this article, about flying. Said we've become just like cattle. We keep trusting our lives to people we don't even know. Like pilots."

He stood up, pushing the stool back, and slid along toward the cash register.

She scuttled quickly after him. "Like pilots, for instance. Said we do it all the time, the article did. And just as often as not, get our heads bashed in for being so trusting." They arrived at the register together. He handed her the check, and she rang it up. "You ever think about that?"

"Yeah." He let his eyes roam to the back where, behind a glass partition, was a betting parlor.

"Like those pilots I date. Hell, this article said that half those guys are so snockered they don't even know what button to press. What you think o' that?"

A large chalkboard was hung high on one wall of the betting parlor, the hastily scrawled entries and their ac companying odds barely legible from where Ben stood. His eyes wandered over the board.

"I mean, one minute you're flying at thirty thousand feet, the next—boom!—you're splattered all over the ground," she spaced her words here with practiced clarity, "with somebody's dachshund nibbling at your pancreas."

Suddenly his eyes riveted on one of the entries on the board. He took a couple of steps toward the glass.

"Hey, mister, you want your change?"

He turned to her, his mind still on the chalkboard. "You say something?"

"Yeah." She was sulky. "I asked if you wanted your change."

He held out his hand, and she dropped some singles and change into it. He started for the betting parlor.

"Listen," she called after him, "you want my opinion, flying *sucks!*"

The sports book was a strictly utilitarian affair, a long counter fronted with grillwork windows that separated the bookies' alley from the ranks of betting customers. Shockley entered the room and looked again at the large board bearing the Vegas "line" on various events, horse racing accounting for the majority of the listings.

He quickly spotted what he was looking for, and was a bit unnerved to verify that he hadn't misread the entry from his distance in the bar. The tenth race at Santa Anita, a horse by the name of Mally-No-Show. And the odds were fifty-to-one.

It had to be a coincidence, he kept telling himself as he made his way among milling customers toward the lines at the windows, had to be. Broad probably knew she could rattle him this way.

There were two rows of shuffling customers, and he took a place at the end of the shorter. He kept his eyes on the board.

Finally he was at the counter. A harried bookie with a mustard stain on his tie blinked at him through steel-rimmed glasses. "How much on what, sport?"

"I'm… unh… not sure," Ben mumbled.

"Well, this is the betting line, fella. Not the make-up-your-mind line."

"Yeah." Ben barely heard the bookie's answer; he was occupied with watching a runner erase the odds next to Mally-No-Show and replace them with a quote of sixty-to-one.

"Well?" the bookie prodded. "Let's have it."

Ben felt customers behind him pushing in. "What's the story on that horse there, Mally-No-Show?"

"Story? Sixty-to-one is the story."

"Yeah, yeah. I can read. What's her record? What races has she run before?"

The bookie pursed his lips and pushed a sigh through them. "Look, buddy, I don't know shit from horses. I don't train, I don't buy, I don't ride. I just put the names on the board. What you see is what you get. As for that one, this morning she opened at twenty-to-one and the house has been raising the odds ever since, most of it in the last couple hours. You're a first-timer, eh? Okay. The smart dough must figure she ain't got a chance. So that's the story. You want to make a bet or not?"

Ben heard a muttered "Come on!" behind him.

"No," he said. "No, I guess not."

Walking back to the police station, he found himself unable to shift his mind from pondering the entry and its astronomical odds. Sixty-to-one. And they'd tripled in just the few hours since morning, most of it just since his own arrival in Vegas.

What the hell was going on? For the first time in his adult life, he wished he was a gambler, wished he knew more than basic cop info on odds and sudden changes and smart money.

He wished he'd been to the track a few times and seen a few tout sheets and a few horses' names. Then maybe he would have heard of this mare or filly or whatever the hell she was, and he wouldn't have the nagging pinprick in the back of his mind needling him that what Mally had said might be the truth. He wouldn't even consider the ridiculous idea that there *was* a line out against his ever bringing Augustina, a.k.a. Gus, Mally back to testify at some piss-ant trial that was apparently none of his business anyway.

But none of this could be real. Who'd give a rat's ass

whether a Vegas whore recited her entire life history from a witness stand in Phoenix, Arizona? What could she possibly know that was so incriminating? That she fucked somebody for dough? Christ, nobody cares about that. Half the force, including himself... Well, what could it be?

Nothing. He decided, said it aloud, "Nothing." There just wasn't enough there to worry about. He'd take her back, report to Blakelock all neat and tidy, and carry on with his life.

It was that simple.

Should be that simple.

Still...

A block from the police station he passed a public phone booth on a corner. Silently cursing his own weakness on the matter, he went back to the booth. He closed the folding door, flipped open the yellow pages of the directory, drew his finger under a name, dropped a dime in the slot and dialed.

A brisk male voice answered. "Ed's Pony Book."

"Yeah, I want to check on a horse named Mally-No-Show, tenth at Santa Anita. You got a line on her?"

"Hang on a minute." After a brief pause, "Sure thing, pal. We got her. You can have her. Seventy-to-one."

"Seventy?" Shockley took a breath. "Fifteen minutes ago it was sixty-to-one."

"So? Aren't you glad you waited? But don't stretch your luck. The odds are bound to go down. Bet it now. No filly can be *that* bad."

Ben slammed the receiver down and wrenched open the door to the booth. His intellect told him to forget the whole thing. His gut told him he was in trouble.

CHAPTER 5

Mally's first look at Shockley as he entered her cell told her something had happened to change his mind.

"You found out I was right, didn't you?"

"I didn't find out shit," he snapped. "All I know is there's a horse named Mally-No-Show running in the tenth race at Santa Anita, and from the way the odds are climbing, someone must figure she's gonna drop dead at the goddam gate."

"That's what I've been trying to tell you!" She slammed her palm against the cell wall. "*This* is the gate. Right *here* in *Vegas!* Why can't you wake up something in that fuzz brain of yours? Look at it! They're saying we haven't got a chance! Jesus, what does it take to get through to you?"

"For all I know it's a real horse, just a coincidence, a fluke."

"Sure, Shockley," she hissed, "a coincidence!" She swept up her blanket and flung it against the wall. "Well, here's another coincidence, fella: *there isn't any tenth race at Santa Anita!"*

He had already turned his attention toward two strapping young paramedics who were opening the cell door. Mally sank down on the cot and buried her face in her hands. She wished she could cry, but this ability had left her long ago, along with the ability to laugh honestly.

The taller of the two paramedics stepped inside the door.

"Your wagon's outside," he said to Ben.

"Good. Did you check on that horse?"

"Seventy-five-to-one," the other paramedic answered.

"Sounds like a real nag. What's that all about?"

"Nothing." Ben's face tightened.

Mally watched him. "Listen, Shockley, you hear him? You better call it off. Please call it off." Her voice was pleading, soft. "Leave me here. Get outta here, go back home, tell 'em something. I'll work it out from my end. You're calling their hand, Shockley, and they got all the cards. *Please!"* She searched for understanding behind his coal-hard eyes but found nothing. Her words were drawing a blank. She wasn't one to beg. If only he knew her better, knew how much it hurt her to plead for anything, then he'd understand...

"We're leaving," Ben said to the paramedics. *"Now.* One of you, get me a car, rental, go call Hertz, Avis, National—I don't give a damn who. But get me a car. Have it waiting halfway between here and the airport, on some side street, with the keys in it. Tell 'em to drop the car and beat it; I'll take responsibility. I'll pay for it as soon as she sets foot on the plane. Here, take down my shield number and give it to 'em." He held out his shield. The taller paramedic rummaged in his pants pocket for a scrap of paper, and wrote it down. "Get on it!"

The paramedic nodded and trotted out.

"You're killing us both," Mally said dully. "I hope to hell you realize that. But if your mentality is standard fuzz, you won't believe me until you see blood."

Shockley looked at her, his lean face stony. The other paramedic shuffled nervously in the corridor. Ben rubbed a finger behind his ear and studied Mally's unsmiling face. "If —and I say *if*—what you've been saying is true," he said slowly, "then that means somebody out there is betting I can't do my job. Well, they're full of shit. Anybody that's been betting that line for fifteen years has lost a bundle."

"You crazy, brainless bastard!" She was on her feet, fists clenched at her sides. "The people laying those odds are gonna chew you up and spit you out! You're fucking insane! You can't bluff your way out of this, or just flash your goddam badge! They're gonna laugh at you, right while they're chopping you up! And me with you! I'm not going *anywhere* with you!"

She hurled herself down on the cot, clinging to its metal frame with a white-knuckled grip, burying her face in the thin mattress, her eyes shut tight against the tears of defeat and fear that flooded them.

Shockley stared at her for a moment, feeling neither sympathy nor contempt. But his usually steady nerves jangled with the intensity of her words, with the implications. He realized that there had been too many jobs, too many directives blindly obeyed.

But there was a secondary moment, as he looked at her, when he felt torn. If she was intent on mere survival, he was no less so. He was loyal and dedicated, but not suicidally so.

He wasn't into laying down his life, not for her, not even for his job.

But he also realized that now the job was all that he had left. Being a cop was often a one-step-at-a-time thing, a spontaneous application of judgments propelling you through the labyrinth of a case. That was how you survived in a business that had no script. His job was what he was told to do: how he did it was up to him, one step at a time.

Whatever the odds, you beat them and staggered through.

That was what kept him from feeling like a flunky, a gofer: the fact that what you were told to accomplish was only the final result; how you achieved it was up to you.

His thoughts lasted only the briefest part of an instant.

What he was left with was this conviction: he was on the job now, and if he gave it up he knew that whatever Ben Shockley was would cease to exist.

And given what he knew, there was no alternative. He turned his cold eyes to the remaining paramedic, nodded, and together they advanced toward the prostrate girl on the cot.

The heavy door at the rear of the women's detention wing swung open, and sunlight from the alley flooded the dimly lit access corridor.

Shockley lowered his eyes at the sudden burst of light but kept moving, his hands behind his back gripping the foot end of a lightweight gurney that bore his prisoner.

Gus Malley lay on her back, muffled noises of protest issuing from beneath her gag, her body twisting against the nylon restraining straps.

The taller paramedic stood in the alley beside the waiting ambulance, watching his partner and Shockley descend the short ramp with their cargo. A few seconds later they slid the gurney into the rear of the ambulance.

Then Ben turned to the waiting paramedic. "What's the story on the rent-a-car?"

"Seventy-five Plymouth. Blue. License..." The man dug into his pocket for the crumpled piece of paper. "License C55205. It'll be parked just off the Strip, on Logan. They had some questions, but—"

"Okay. Now, who's the driver of this wagon?"

"Right here." The paramedic who had helped him carry the gurney raised a hand.

"Then let's go."

The driver slammed the bay doors of the ambulance closed, then hurried around to the left side and slid into the driver's seat. Ben and the other men started for the passenger side. Ben pushed him aside and swung open the door. "Not you, just the driver."

"Hey, what the hell are you doing?" The man reached for the door as Shockley banged it shut. "We're a *team.*"

"Not unless you plan on running alongside, you're not." He rapped the dashboard with his fist. "Let's roll!"

The bewildered driver hesitated, glanced out at his partner, then shoved the ambulance into gear and sent it screeching down the alley.

As soon as they were underway, Ben scrambled over the seat, knelt beside the gurney, and began untying Mally's gag.

"Hit the bells!" he called to the driver, who flipped a toggle switch and brought the siren wailing to life.

A barrage of insults poured from Mally the instant the gag was off. "Cheap-shot gutless bastard! You really get it off roughing up girls, don't you, you cocksucker! Big man! Big forty-five-caliber fairy!"

"Yeah," Ben said wearily, "that's me."

"You and your shit-head macho mentality! You stupid rummy cop! You'll get us both blown away before—"

He jammed an oxygen mask over her nose and mouth.

She struggled. He reached behind him and gave a quarter turn on the tank valve. "Breathe deep." He crouched over her as if he were a concerned physician administering to his patient.

Quickly she began to feel the effects of the gas upon her system, and though her rage was undiminished, she forced herself under control, hoping that he'd remove the mask.

In a moment, he lifted it from her face, still holding it close. Their eyes locked.

She breathed heavily, glaring up at him. It took an enormous effort to stifle the new barrage of curses she wanted to shout. There was always some word, some tidy insult, some twist of the verbal blade, that wounded a man effectively.

But she was silent, except for her panting breath. Only her eyes spoke.

Finally he hung the mask beside the tank and turned off the valve. Their antagonism fairly crackled beneath the cover of the siren. They looked at each other, Mally trying to penetrate the icy calm of her captor, Shockley working hard to avoid the questions that raced through his head.

Her mouth moved wordlessly. Then, aloud, "Why?"

The stark validity of the one-word question reached him, causing the tone of his eyes to alter slightly. "Because it's my job."

"No." She shook her head. "People don't commit suicide for their jobs. Not sane ones, anyway. Not your kind of people."

"Cops get themselves killed all the time."

"Sure. In the heat of an argument. In the middle of a battle. Busting up a fight. Breaking down a door. But not like this. Not just out of blind stubbornness. Unless they're totally dumb. I can't believe you're that totally dumb."

"Haven't you been telling me all along that we're in a war? A war against the people who want you dead?"

"They only want me dead if I leave Vegas with you. I stay here and keep my nose clean, they don't give a shit. So we're still in Vegas. Nothing's started yet, Shockley. It's all up to you. Just tell your driver to pull over. We'll just wave goodbye. Bygones will be bygones. Let me walk away from here, and nothing happens. To either of us."

"I can't do that." Shockley felt trapped into giving answers in the kind of exchange where he should just keep his mouth shut—first rule of cop procedures.

"Because of your precious job."

"That's right." Why was he responding to her? Because of his doubts? Because he wanted her to keep talking, to somehow convince him, one way or the other?

"Bullshit. That's not half the answer. You're not even

arresting me, Shockley. I'm not even a *suspect* to you. You don't even know what's going down. You're nothing but a runner for the P.D., picking up and dropping off. No, that's not your job. And if I thought I was going to live long enough, I'd probably be able to find out the *real* reason."

The ambulance swerved into an unexpected left turn, throwing Ben off balance. Then the driver cut the siren and slowed to a stop.

He leaned back over the seat and pointed across the street.

"There's your car, officer."

Ben glanced through the windshield and saw a blue Plymouth parked opposite them, against the far curb, its license plate bearing the number he'd memorized back in the alley.

"Okay," he barked at the driver. "Hop out and get it, bring it alongside here. I'll get her ready for the transfer."

The paramedic jumped out and trotted across the street while Shockley removed Mally's lower restraining strap.

Mally lay stiffly, but as he worked on the upper restraint he couldn't ignore the raw emotions in her eyes. And the second she was free her hands were a blur of pummeling fists and clawing fingernails. "Son of a bitch!" she screamed. "To hell with you and your fucking badge! Go die alone! Waste your fucking life! But don't take me with you!"

He threw himself across her flailing arms and felt her teeth sink into his right shoulder—the possibility flashed through his mind that she might actually bite through the fabric. As he wrestled to get her under control, he heard the Plymouth's engine turning over.

A fraction of a second later an incredible light flashed over them; he and Mally were slammed to the floor of the ambulance by a violent concussion; the Plymouth disintegrated in an explosion of orange flame and swirling blue steel.

CHAPTER 6

Mally felt the crush of Shockley's body against her, heard the unnatural rain of glass and metal peppering the ambulance, and saw the wave of searing flame rising outside the windshield. She was paralyzed.

Ben scrambled to his feet and dove for the driver's seat.

Mally instinctively tried to follow him. She barely had time to raise herself to her quaking knees before he had started the engine, whacked the shift arm into gear, and spun the ambulance away from the curb and around the corner.

She was thrown backwards, against the rear door. She pulled herself up to the window. Her mouth hung open, her eyes widened in disbelief at the brief but vivid tableau of the flaming, gutted Plymouth, the paramedic's torso hanging like a torn rag doll from the gaping hole where the door had been.

Siren screaming, the ambulance weaved and dodged its way through the afternoon traffic, causing Mally to grab hold of the back of the passenger seat to keep from being thrown back and forth against the sides. Before she could speak, Shockley reached beneath his coat, took out his Magnum, and handed it back to her, never taking his eyes off the road.

Mally peered dumbly at the blue-black weapon that hovered in front of her in his outstretched hand.

"Come on!" he barked. "Take it!"

"What's that for?" Her mind felt as if it were jammed with cotton.

"It's a fucking *gun!* Take it!"

"No." She was dazed, confused. "I don't want it."

"Goddam it! You'll take it, *now!*"

Nauseated, dizzy, she gingerly took the gun in her two hands and stared at the back of Ben's head.

"Aim it out the back window!" Shockley commanded. "Anyone follows us—shoot!"

"Anyone?" Her voice was a faint whisper. She sagged to the floor. "I can't shoot anybody."

"Wake up, will you?" He swerved the wheel violently to pass a car. "That was supposed to be *us* in that Plymouth back there, and they're gonna carry away what's left of that poor bastard in a plastic bag! You wanna be next?"

"No." It was not an answer; she was speaking to the gun, staring at it. She remained immobile. The ambulance veered sharply to the right, sending her tumbling into the wall.

"Okay," she whispered. Her right hand shaped itself around the gun-grip, her index finger looping unsteadily on the trigger. "Okay," her lips said. She inched on her knees to the rear window. The flow of traffic behind them was sparse. But it was threatening. And as she looked at the blur of cars and black asphalt, the realization that the war was now real settled slowly into her.

Until then it had been all theory, supposition, logic. Despite her earlier convictions of its coming, her intense and visceral fears of what might lie ahead, it had not been real.

Not real like this. It was as if she had suffered from the same blindness of which she had accused Ben: until there was blood, there was no war.

Now it was different; combat was underway, the first life

had already been lost. Ironically, it was Ben who had grasped it first, had been able to react to it, had launched the first defensive maneuvers. She had been too stunned to move. It was real; now the logic was that the war wouldn't end until she was dead.

Shockley careened onto a side street, slamming her again into the wall and at the same time snapping her out of her paralyzing reverie.

"Where the hell are you going?" she yelled.

"Trying to take a less popular way to the airport. If I can find one."

She thought his voice too calm. "After what happened back *there?* They'll be *waiting* for us at the airport, for chrissake!"

"Not if they think we're dead. By the time they sift through that wreckage we'll be thirty thousand feet up."

Mally thought carefully, quickly, mustering her wits and her will to survive, assessing the situation for a way out. Her decision came fast, numbed her. She looked at the gun, then turned and aimed it squarely at Shockley's head. "Pull over."

Ben glanced in the rear-view mirror and saw the barrel of the gun homing in unsteadily on the base of his right ear. He switched his eyes back to the road, the ambulance continuing its wailing flight.

"I said pull over. Do it now." Her voice was calmer, the gun steadier in her hand.

"I'm doing fifty miles an hour," Ben said tersely. "Until you pull that trigger, we're heading for the airport."

"You that anxious to die?"

"No more than you are, and that's what we'll both do if you blow my head off at this speed. And what we may do if we stop."

She tried to swallow; her mouth was cardboard dry. "I mean it, Shockley. I swear to Christ, if you don't stop this thing—"

A sudden *thunk* hit the rear window and the windshield at tire same time, cutting off her words. The bullet had passed clear through the ambulance.

"Drop!" Ben yelled.

Mally reflexively hit the deck. "What the hell's going on?" she cried.

"They're shooting at us! Get back there and return their fire!"

"Oh, my Christ!" Keeping low, Mally scrambled to the rear doors. She peeked out of the punctured window where spidery cracks radiated outward from a neat, round bullet hole.

"Shoot!" Shockley's command echoed in the ambulance.

Her eyes fixed on the black car following them, matching their every turn and maneuver. "I think it's the police!"

"It's not the goddam police! *I'm* the police! Now use the gun!"

"I can't!"

"Bitch! You were ready to shoot *me!*"

Was she? She didn't really know. She'd never even had a gun in her hands before. Could she shoot somebody? To live, she could. Maybe, if...

A second bullet thudded into the doors less than a foot away, and Mally stopped thinking.

She raised the gun to the rear window, steadying the heavy Magnum in both slender hands, gritted her teeth, sighted, then closed her eyes and fired three bone-jolting shots in rapid succession.

The windshield of the black car was blown into a cloud of splintered glass, flying shards lacerating the driver and his passenger. The vehicle skidded out of control, veered across the sidewalk, and hurtled through a storefront.

Mally stared at it, awed. "I hit it! I hit it!" The threat to her life having quickly vanished, she was exhilarated. Then the fact of what she'd done struck like an aftershock. "Oh, my

God," she moaned softly. She crept backwards towards the front seat, stunned, staring.

The moment she was near enough, Shockley reached back over the seat, snatched the gun from her shaking hands, and jammed it into his belt.

The gun. Her only means of survival. The gun had saved her. She threw herself at him in a desperate frenzy, clawing at his arm and grappling for the gun which had kept her alive. Screams of fury punctuated her attack as she tumbled over the passenger seat, her arms locked around his neck in a choke hold.

His throat closing from the pressure, her forearm covering his eyes, he reached to break her grip, and felt the unguided ambulance lurch to the right and jump the curb.

A pedestrian dove onto a lawn as the berserk machine clipped off a pair of lampposts. Shockley lunged at the wheel with his left hand as he threw a hard right elbow into Mally's ribcage.

The blow sent her slamming into the passenger door, her hand instinctively grabbing the handle for support. The door opened before she knew what she was doing, flinging wide, drawing her with it.

She tumbled half out, clutching wildly at the flapping door as it pulled her from the seat. Her agonized scream was drowned out by the violent rush of air that whipped at her and threatened to tear her from the car.

CHAPTER 7

Mally dangled in the wind, only her feet still inside the compartment, her hand clinging to the slippery chrome door handle.

Shockley fought for control of the ambulance, which bore down on an iron guardrail only a few short yards from the onrushing open door.

Wrenching the wheel savagely over with his left hand, he lunged to his right, grabbed the belt of Mally's prison dress, and pulled with all his might.

There was an instant of crackling, popping threads as the garment started to give way. He thought he'd lose her. But then her body yielded to his pull, and she thudded safely in against him just as the free-swinging door was ripped from the side of the car and clattered off behind them.

The sound of tearing metal ringing in her ears, Mally stared through shock-induced calm at the empty space beside her, where the door had been, where she had been.

Then, in a daze, she groped behind the seat for her hand bag, found it, took out her brush, and began to draw it through her hair with firm, steady strokes.

The ambulance under control at last, Shockley looked at her and shook his head.

She stared straight ahead and continued brushing.

Her mind held only dimly the fact that he'd saved her life; till then she'd thought him the one who would lose it. Their interdependence was not something she could grasp or admit.

For a minute they drove on in silence, and their heavy breathing subsided.

"Okay," Ben said finally, softly, "forget the airport. But where else? I'll be damned if I know anywhere else to go." It sounded weak to him, like they were on a goddam date or something. He waited for her curses and insults.

"Six blocks down," she said calmly. "Hang a left. Second house in, on the right. The garage will be open."

She gave the instructions routinely, never missing a stroke with her brush. For the first time, he looked at her with something that might have passed for respect. Or even gratitude.

The house was a wooden-frame, two-story structure of neo-Victorian design, with peeling yellow paint and a flimsy, leaning front porch. It was located in a dreary neighbourhood south of the strip, an area of other ramshackle homes and overgrown vacant lots.

Shockley turned in the driveway and maneuvered the ambulance into a decaying garage at the rear of the house. He switched off the engine and leaned his head back against the seat, letting out a small sigh of relief.

Mally slid immediately out of her door, stopped to replace the hairbrush in her purse, and headed for the back porch.

Ben stepped from the ambulance, pulled the warped, paint-flaked garage door shut, and caught up with her at the back door.

Reaching up to a molding, she took a key from atop the

sill and turned it in the tarnished lock. The door creaked open, and she stared inside.

"Hold it." He motioned her back outside. "Wait right here."

He started off toward the side of the house, then an after thought: "No, no, come with me."

She followed him. He made a quick survey outside the house. At the front, he looked up and down the street. There were no cars, no sign of any life. "Anybody living in any of these houses?"

"Not the closer ones. Both sides of this house here are vacant. Somebody living four houses down, I think."

He nodded and went around to the back again. "Okay." He waved her through the door and followed her in.

Mally strode casually through a service area where rusted, capped pipes stood ready for a washer hook-up, into the kitchen where their footsteps on the yellowed linoleum were echoed by the steady drip-drip-drip of a faucet, down a short hallway with faded wallpaper, and into a severe, sparsely furnished bedroom.

Once Shockley was inside the room, she gave a quick kick to the door, swinging it shut.

He took in the room at a glance—double bed, covered with a bright purple sheet; three-drawer dresser; a single nightstand holding a phone with pushbuttons indicating two lines; mirrors, one at the head of the bed extending to the ceiling, another, about half the size of the bed, fixed flat to the ceiling. He knew precisely what it was. A quizzical smile crossed his face. "Who'd need a rundown freelance cathouse in Vegas?"

She shrugged. "Locals, mostly," she said matter-of-factly.

"Married men cheating on their wives. Guys who aren't supposed to be in town. That sort of thing." There was no trace of shame in her voice, but there was a trace of challenge. She arched her eyebrows and cocked her head, looking at him.

He reached down for the phone and dialed quickly, still standing, without taking his eyes off Mally.

She moved to the dresser, dabbing at her hair and watching him in the mirror.

He waited anxiously for the connection to go through, then spoke with staccato rapidity. "Internal Affairs, Lieutenant Commander Blakelock."

There was a lingering pause, then Blakelock's deformed basso thundered in Ben's ear. "Shockley? What the hell? You were supposed to be on the plane fifteen minutes ago!"

"I'm holed up," Ben answered bluntly. "Seems someone doesn't want your 'nothing' witness to testify at your 'nothing' trial."

There was a pause. "Don't be absurd."

"Somebody blew up our car. Somebody took some shots at us. I think we shook 'em all, whoever it was. So I'm holed up."

"Why would anyone… it doesn't make any sense."

"Not to me it doesn't. But it must to somebody, 'cause it's already cost some people. Listen, I'm going to need help if you want her alive."

"Well, I don't know what—"

"Call the Vegas police. Tell them to send a couple of black-and-whites. I'll use one as a decoy, take the other to the airport."

"What flight?"

"I don't know yet; whatever is ready to roll."

"Where are you?"

"Unh…" He looked at Mally's reflection in the mirror. "Where the hell are we?"

"Two-oh-three Rothdell," she said.

"Two-oh-three Rothdell, south side, old two-story yellow place. Cathouse."

"Cathouse?"

"Her office." He saw her scowl in the mirror.

"Okay," Blakelock grunted. "Keep your ass right there, don't move. Understand?"

"Of course I'll stay here. Where the hell else can I go?"

"I... the department... we're counting on you to bring that witness in... Don't like these delays... We can't afford any screw-ups."

"Yessir. Kind of screw-ups we're having, I can't afford, either."

The connection went dead, and Ben hung up. Mally turned from the dresser and looked at him. "Sounds like you've got it wired. One-two-three."

"Let's put it this way—with a little luck, it should work."

"Should?"

"Will. It's my life, too, you know."

"Okay, Shockley," she sighed. "I guess you win. I'm too tired to fight it any more. I'll go along peacefully."

He sat down on the edge of the bed. "Glad to hear it."

"You've done everything you promised, except shoot me."

"You haven't tried to run yet."

She moved over to the bed, looking down at him. "You ever shoot anybody?"

"Nope."

"I'm one up on you."

He widened his eyes.

"That car back there."

"Oh, yeah."

"At least I shot at the car. I don't know if I could actually shoot a person."

"I could."

"Let's not talk about shooting any more." Her voice was softer.

"Okay."

"Listen," she said haltingly, "this isn't all that easy for me to say, but, well, I appreciate what you did back there. In the ambulance, I mean. If you hadn't pulled me back in—"

"My job is to deliver you—in one piece."

"I know. Still, I owe you." She lay back across the bed, staring up into the overhead mirror, her firm breasts pressing against the denim prison dress. "Are you married?"

"No." He didn't look at her.

"Divorced?"

"I forget."

"Any kids? Family?"

"What do you care?"

"I'm interested in you."

"Why?" Was he glad she was, if she was?

"You're not exactly a run-of-the-mill cop."

"Yeah. How did you put it? An on-the-ropes bum."

"Jailhouse talk." She sat up, her body lightly brushing his. "So I made a mistake. I was scared."

"And you're not any more?"

She smiled. "How about a cigarette?"

He took a pack from his shirt pocket, shook them loose, and held them out to her. She took one. He lit it with a disposable lighter.

She took a deep drag, tilted her head toward the ceiling, and watched the smoke curl up to flatten out against the mirror. Then she set a cigarette in an ashtray on the night stand, slowly tucking it into the notched rim. She leaned forward next to him. Reaching across to his lap, she gently picked up one of his hands and held it between her own. She moved her fingertips across its hard, sinewy contours. "Ever been read?"

"What?"

"Ever had your palm read?"

"No. Shit."

"You've got strong hands," she said softly. "Every woman's

got her 'thing' about men, you know. Something that turns them on. With me, it's hands—like yours."

He looked at her, studying her. There was a certain softness. He wondered about the small scar on her mouth. She undid one button on her dress, then gently lifted his hand and put it inside on her breast.

He cupped the breast in his hand, traced the nipple with his thumb.

"Come on." Her voice was an urgent whisper. "We've got time. We've earned it."

Slowly she pushed him back on the bed, following his descent with soft, teasing kisses which he didn't resist. "We'll have a good time," she murmured. "Such a good time."

She kissed him hard on the mouth, working her tongue between his lips. She slid her hand to the inside of his thigh and caressed it softly. "Just lie there, baby. Mama'll do all the work. You're beautiful. *So* beautiful."

Her dress riding higher with each movement, she moved her hips back and forth against his leg, her rhythm increasing in tempo.

In time she felt the bulge of his response. She worked on it, stimulated it, increased it.

Suddenly her caressing fingers darted from his thigh to his waist, to the Magnum that protruded from beneath his belt.

Shockley's hand was already there, a firm grip on the gun.

She snatched her hand away and rolled harshly off him, her teeth bared in anger.

"Somehow," he said, sitting up and smiling ironically, "I get the feeling your heart's not in your work."

CHAPTER 8

"Bastard!" Mally sat up, buttoning her blouse, not looking at him.

"Why? Just because I wouldn't let you shoot me?"

"Bastard." She stood up and paced. "You know I wouldn't do that. I told you. I don't think I could shoot anybody."

"You've told me a lot of things, honeybunch."

"I just want out of here."

"We *are* getting out, just as soon as the police show up."

"Cops!" she hissed. "One cop, then more cops. Cops solve everybody's problems. Listen, big smart cop. I'll tell you something. You can drag me across the whole goddam country if you want, but I'm not testifying at any trial. I won't open my mouth. They couldn't *beat* it outta me."

"That's fine with me. My job is just to get you there."

She whirled on him, fists clenched, chest heaving. "Your job! Like a damn wind-up toy; wind him up and he says, 'job, job, job.' Is that why you're risking your neck for something as stupid as this? Isn't there more to your life than your fucking job?"

"I do what I'm told." He was sorry he said it.

"So does an *imbecile.* Or a damn *slave.* Worst thing in the world is an imbecile slave. Give it a rest, for chrissake! You got a mind like a music box! She turned away from him and folded her arms, muttering more words he could not hear.

He reached for the phone and dialed information, the operator's cheery voice a poor accompaniment for his mood.

"I need the listing for Air West," he said.

"One moment, please."

While he was waiting, staring through the gauzy curtains at the window, he saw the tops and waving antennas of the two black-and-whites as they pulled into the driveway.

The operator came back on and gave him the number. He repeated it once to lodge it in his memory and hung up.

Mally had turned towards the window at the sound of the approaching cars. Now she stared apprehensively in their direction.

"Time to go," Shockley said. He got up from the bed and smoothed his clothes.

"Do you mind?" she asked, gesturing toward the open door of the bathroom. "Once we're in the air, I'd hate to have you worry that I might jump out of the washroom window."

"One window's as good as another," he said. He brushed past her to the bathroom and satisfied himself that there was no means of escape. The only access to the outside was a small, crank-operated window that could open only a few inches because of the protective iron grillwork behind it.

He stepped back past her into the bedroom. "Go ahead. Just don't take all day."

She walked in and shut the door behind her.

He dialed the airline number.

Outside, another pair of squad cars rolled quietly up to the house. Shockley, on the phone making arrangements for the return flight, didn't notice them. He was likewise oblivious to the arrival of yet a third contingent—two cars and a tactical van that pulled into position diagonally across from the house.

He hung up the phone, walked over to the bathroom door, and rapped sharply on it. "Let's go."

There was no answer. He thumped with the side of his fist.

"Hey, come on. We got a plane to catch." He twisted the doorknob. Locked. "Come on, dammit! Open the fucking door before I blow it open!"

No answer. No sound.

He backed off two paces and drew his gun, preparing to shoot the lock, when an amplified voice boomed through the bedroom window.

"You in the house! Come out with your hands on top of your heads!"

Shockley was stunned, disbelieving. For an instant he stared at the window, staring after the sound. Then, crouching close to the floor, he scurried across and peered out the side of the curtains.

What he saw baffled and scared him. The officers from the original pair of squad cars, those he had seen arrive, were deployed in the classic attack formation: kneeling behind their black-and-whites, guns trained over tire hoods and trunks directly at the bedroom window from which he saw them.

Still keeping low, he ran to the front entrance of the house, flattened himself against the door jamb, and cautiously edged the door open a crack.

This view was even more astonishing than the other: two more squad cars and a tactical van. After fifteen years on the bricks, he was instantly aware of the firepower the scene implied.

He eased the door shut, his mind racing frantically for a logical explanation for what was happening.

Then the bullhorn voice boomed again from the street.

"The house is surrounded! Throw out your weapons and surrender! Bring the girl with you!"

Explanations didn't matter, not right then. He had to get out there, Mally with him. Plenty of time for explanations.

But now the whole inexplicable thing had to be defused.

Mally.

The bullhorn: "You have thirty seconds! Starting… *now!*"

The fucking house was about to become a death trap.

CHAPTER 9

Shockley raced back through the hall to the bedroom and launched himself against the locked bathroom door, assaulting it with his fists and feet. "Open the goddam door! Those idiots outside are ready to blow us apart!"

"TWENTY SECONDS!" came the disembodied voice.

"Cunt!" He hurled his shoulder against the door, again and again. "Open the fucking door, bitch!"

The door held firm. He drew his Magnum, stepped back, and fired downward into the doorknob, reducing it to a blob of twisted metal. He finished the job with the heel of his shoe and leaped into the bathroom.

Mally was gone.

Impossible.

But that was not now his major problem. It hit him instantly. His reflexes had betrayed him. The single shot he'd fired would naturally trigger the rest. He leaned back against the bathroom wall, waiting for the second or two that would bring it.

Outside the commander heard Shockley's shot. "We're being fired upon! Return fire, men!"

A score of men quickly leaned forward and sighted.

The first rounds shattered the glass of the bedroom

window and slashed through the flimsy curtains, imbedding themselves in the plaster walls with powdery explosions.

Shockley heard the echoes of shots striking all through the house.

The empty bathroom. She got out of there somehow.

There was no exit. But somehow…

Another barrage slammed into the old house, deafening him. Bullets gouged away at rotten wood and ricocheted off interior walls and fixtures; bulbs shattered; electric wires split under the plaster hissed and sparked; doors splintered.

It was a cacophony straight from hell. Shockley, helpless, terrified, found release in a bellow of primal despair: "MAAALLLYYY!"

Tear gas canisters rocketed into the bedroom, discharging their noxious fumes with muffled *whumps,* the smoke-like gas curling into the air like thick swamp mist and obscuring the view of the bed where only minutes before Shockley had lain enjoying the gentle caresses of a woman, where he had lain in complete, calculating control of the whole situation. But now he was cornered game, cornered by his own species right down to the basic blue, and fighting for his life.

Spinning around in the tiny space of the bathroom, he lashed out at faucets, towel bars, anything that might possibly trigger the route to Mally's escape.

Nothing yielded to his pushing and pulling, and now he felt the beginnings of the burning, choking, stomach-churning effects of the tear gas.

Another salvo hurtled into the tired old house, shaking it to its foundation.

Ben hit the deck as the glass in the bathroom window blew inward in a hail of flying shards. Then he heard the sickening groan of wrenching nails and wood, and the splinter of collapsing pillars as the porticoed front porch sagged, hung suspended, and finally collapsed in a heap on the ground, its supporting beams and rafters shredded by the fury of the attack.

Flames sprang up from the exploding canisters that continued to assault the bedroom, and the stench of the burning mattress mingled with the thick, acrid smoke.

Coughing, gagging, his eyes a watery, stinging blur, Shockley struggled to his feet. Pressing a handkerchief against his nose and mouth, he continued to grope for the freedom that Mally had already found. He stumbled against the tub, an old-fashioned, claw-footed affair set some two or three feet from the wall.

The tub gave against his weight, moving just enough to expose part of a narrow crawl-hole in the floor beneath it.

He heaved quickly against the tub, sliding it farther away, his clouded vision barely able to perceive the wooden stairs leading down to the blackness beneath the house.

His lungs aching, he began an unsteady descent into what he hoped would be clear air and the way to safety.

As the ongoing fusillade cannonaded again through the house just above him, eerie thoughts flashed through his mind.

Running from the cops, desperately, for his life.

Innocent.

Was this what it was like, then, to be hunted by men just like him?

Would it be any less terrifying, any more tolerable, if he were guilty of a crime?

He had never in his fifteen years as a cop comprehended the devastating fear that must ravage those fleeing from the cops.

The cellar extended under the entire ground floor of the house. What little light filtered down from the crawl-hole was soon dissipated into angular shadows that quickly gave way to deep, almost impenetrable darkness.

And even the crawl-hole was becoming clouded with gas.

It seemed to be following him down, like an evil spirit.

Ben stood at the foot of the stairs, steadying himself against the wooden railing as he gasped for air. His chest throbbed from his violent coughing, and he thought his stomach would surely rebel at even the slightest further movement.

But he forced himself to move away from the staircase.

Mally must be in here, someplace.

"Mally?" he called softly. Something collapsed thunderously over his head, and dust from the floorboards drifted down and into his nose. He coughed some more.

He'd gone a few yards when his foot thudded into something that produced a metallic scraping sound against the concrete floor.

He dropped to his knees, felt for the object, bumped it with his fingers. He stared through blood-shot, tearing eyes at the rectangular object.

His eyes could not focus enough. He ran his fingertips over it: a grate.

Then he frantically probed with his hands against the cold, damp floor until he found the opening from which the grate had been removed.

At last his sight was improving, and he could see the patch of jet-black space that indicated the opening of an underground passage.

Certainly Mally had come this way, and it had been she who had moved the grate during her escape.

"Mally?"

But what if the police also knew about the route? What if they had men stationed at its exit, waiting to destroy the first thing that moved from it?

Mally could already be dead, and he might well be on his way to join her. Yet, what other options did he have? If there was a conventional, ground-level exit to the cellar, it was a foregone conclusion that the police had it covered.

Even if he came out in an attitude of surrender, it was too late; they simply couldn't stop shooting in time to spare his life.

That much he knew for a fact. Once, when he was still in uniform, he'd been involved in a heavy assault against a pair of barricaded suspects. He remembered what it felt like, squeezing off round after round: a crazy, numb momentum built up inside him. He couldn't pull the trigger fast enough to satisfy himself. He had wanted to demolish everything in his sightline—house, suspects, cars, shrubbery—anything that stood within range of his gun.

That was what was happening, now, above his own head.

If he was foolish enough to step into it, there was absolutely no chance for survival.

So he could do nothing but follow the passageway and hope that he'd still be alive when he came out the other end.

He leaned into the tunnel to call a final time, "Mally?"

Then, touching his Magnum to make sure it was wedged firmly in place, he swung his legs down into the opening, placed his palms flat against the concrete floor, and let himself slowly down into the black hole.

His feet touched the softness of raw earth just as his head passed below the cellar floor.

A few feet in front of him, the stoutly shored walls and roof of the narrow tunnel disappeared into the darkness.

While he stood waiting for his gas-fatigued eyes to adjust, he thought of Josie's parting comment at the airport.

"We've gone through a lot of doors together," his friend had said.

And so they had: bursting through closed doors, one man standing erect, his gun trained chest-high at whatever might be waiting on the opposite side; the other diving into the room, low to the floor to present a minimum target, his life quite literally in the hands of his covering partner.

How many times had he and Josie done that? More often

than he could remember, or wanted to. And each time it had been an act of pure trust—that whatever you met, you were good enough as a team to come out alive.

Now he had to go through another door, figuratively, but this time there would be no one covering him. This time he was putting his life in his own hands, and if he lost it…

He pushed the thought from his mind and began his journey down the tunnel, holding his gun in front of him and trying not to think what the man would look like, the man who might be waiting at the other end to kill him. Because the man, if he was there, would be wearing a badge.

As he moved slowly forward, the only sounds were his shallow breathing and the shuffling of his feet on the loose dirt. His vision was short and dim, but the passageway seemed soundly enough constructed, and every now and then he'd glance to his right or left at a sturdy beam, reassuring himself that at least his fate wouldn't be to end up buried alive beneath tons of collapsing earth.

He continued on for an interminable five or six minutes. Then, rounding the only bend in an otherwise straight path, he saw the bright glow of daylight far ahead; he was at an intersecting passage. Only this one wasn't homemade. It was a huge circular storm drain.

The far end, where the daylight was, was perhaps two minutes away. A thin film of sweat formed between the palm of his right hand and the grip of his gun.

The ball of sunlight grew larger with each succeeding step, and he felt the years of training and instinct gathering within him, preparing him for… whatever.

About five yards from the mouth of the tunnel, he flattened himself against one wall and edged along it.

He could see now that the exit was partially blocked with heavy vertical bars, but they were for reinforcement rather than restraint, because an average-size person could pass between them with ease.

Squinting against the light, Ben continued his cautious progress, inching forward, ready to open fire at the slightest provocation. His movements were steady, smooth, quiet; he was no more than a yard away from the end.

His senses strained to detect any indication of an ambush.

He sensed nothing.

He decided to make his exit not between the side-most bars, but through the middle, so he could emerge ready to leap in either direction.

Attempting to swallow, but finding only a dry tightness in his throat, he gathered himself, swung between the bars, faked a move to his left, and made a diving roll to his right, coming up sighting over the barrel of his gun. He panned the gun quickly.

He was alone.

Rising slowly erect, the adrenalin still coursing through his body, he took in his surroundings.

He was at the base of the drainage culvert whose slick walls sloped away on either side to a height above his head.

He let out a long, slow breath and started to make his way along the cement-lined valley.

Some yards ahead an angular baffle jutted out into the culvert—a good place for an ambush.

He inched forward again, sighting down his gun. He reached the baffle and stopped. If there was to be an ambush, those planning to carry it out could not have known he was there—they'd have already shot him. He would have been an easy target for the last several minutes.

So he took his time. He drew several silent breaths, then he carefully plotted the exact path his body would take around the baffle and gripped the gun tightly enough to make sure that if he was hit, he could still fire back.

It crossed his mind briefly that he could back off, return the way he had come, and climb the culvert where he had entered it. He might escape the ambush that way.

But no, impossible. They would be watching it, from ground level a few yards away, every inch of it.

He would have to fight his way out of it, right here. He crouched, swaying a bit like a cat, eyed the edge of the baffle, and lunged.

He hit the ground low, legs apart, gun thrust forward at eye level.

Then he froze, stunned.

There, stepping casually into a pair of Levi's, was Augustina Mally.

CHAPTER 10

Hearing him spring out behind her, Mally whirled around.

They stared at each other for a few seconds. Shockley gradually lowered his gun, still gaping at her.

She shrugged and resumed tugging the Levi's up and over her thighs and hips. "I heard the shooting," she said matter-of-factly. "What happened back there?"

"What *happened!* Jesus! All hell happened. You heard it?"

She turned toward him, braless, a freshly laundered blouse unbuttoned over her bare midriff. "It was a little hard to miss."

"I almost didn't get outta there myself, lady. Why the hell didn't you tell me about that bathtub, for chrissake!"

Mally casually buttoned the blouse. "I'm your prisoner, remember? I was trying to escape." She gave him a taunting smile. "You promised to shoot me if I ran. Now's your chance."

"Bang," he said, tucking his gun away.

She snapped the Levi's shut and hiked up the zipper. "Tell me, how is it that a cop winds up running from the cops?"

Ben looked hard at her. "Somebody set me up."

"What do you mean?"

"I mean I was expecting two cars. We got six, and they

blew the house apart. Either they were after me, or they thought it was somebody else in there. Either way, it was a set-up."

"Well, don't blame me, Shockley. It was your idea to call in the cavalry, not mine."

"Yeah." He looked her up and down. "Where'd you get those clothes?"

"Up there." She nodded toward the top of the culvert.

"Somebody's clothesline. So now I'm a thief. You got a right to bust me." She tossed her blonde hair back. "Anyway, I figured half the world had my description by now, so I thought a change of clothes might come in handy."

"Yeah. And that same half of the world is probably chasing both our asses right now. So move."

"You're not still going through with this, are you?" she asked seriously.

"Lady, they can send the fucking United States Army after me, and as far as I'm concerned, it doesn't change my job."

"You're crazy, Shockley. You're still crazy. You don't learn anything. After all that's happened, you're still a numbskull. Who the hell are you trying to impress? Yourself?"

"Maybe. Now, let's get going." He spun her around roughly and gave her a shove forward.

"Where the hell are we going to?"

"First, out of here. Then we'll take it a step at a time."

"Step at a time, all the way to Phoenix?"

"MOVE!"

They hurried along the base of the culvert, tire cement walls tapering high above their heads. Ben checked behind them constantly for any indication that they were being followed.

After two or three minutes of head-ducked scurrying, their knuckles were bloodied from scraping along the walls of the culvert. Mally came to an abrupt, panting stop.

"Keep moving," he ordered.

"You wanna run," she said between gulps of air, "then run."

"You're in no position to argue with me."

"I'm also in no condition to run. So sue me." She drew her arm across her sweating forehead and squatted on the ground, resting her back against the cement.

Shockley looked at her and sighed. He let her rest.

Gradually, the pressure in Mally's chest subsided and the pain in her sides was reduced to a dull ache. Despite being alive after three attempts on her life, she knew she was no better off than when the whole thing had begun. Worse, probably, because after three misses, the other side had to be getting good and damn mad. She had thought earlier that there were actually *three* sides—her, Ben, and them. Now she wasn't sure if she and Ben were just one side.

Thoughtfully, she tilted her face up to him. "Hey, did you shoot at those guys back there? Is that how it started?"

"I didn't do jack-shit."

"Then why? What happened?"

"I told you—somebody set me up."

"Yeah, you told me. But have you thought about it, figured anything out? I mean, do you have any idea what we're going to—"

"Get up. We've rested long enough."

She rose slowly to her feet, her legs rubbery. "So Shockley, do you have an itinerary, or do we just keep running until we die of exhaustion?"

"Up there." He pointed with the gun to the top of the culvert.

"Climb that?" She shook her head. "I'm not a spider, you know."

"Use your hands and feet. Now move."

Reluctantly, Mally bent over until the flat of her hands touched the tilting cement walls, and started up. She slid back twice before finally scrambling to the top and over it.

She lay on the sandy soil, her chest heaving. Ben knelt on one knee, the butt of his Magnum prodding his ribs.

"We need some help," he said.

"You're telling *me.*"

"Is there anyone in this lousy town you can trust?"

"I'm not sure."

"I guess in your line of work you don't exactly make life-long friends."

She sat up, her eyes flashing with indignation. "Knock off that shit, Shockley. You don't know anything about me. And what about you, mister? Those were cops back there, ready to waste you, dude! How many friends do *you* have? Huh?"

She smacked the dirt with her fist. "Come on, who do *you* know that you can trust? Don't talk to me about—"

"Get your ass in gear."

"Bullshit." She flopped back down on her back. "How long do you think you can hide from this thing? You said somebody set you up. Okay. Doesn't that tell you something?"

"It tells me there's a contract out on you, and we can't stay here like we were having a picnic in the park."

"You mean on *us,* a contact on *us.*"

"Okay. *Us.* I believe your story. Satisfied?"

"You believe my story, but you refuse to see what's going on."

"I see. Everything I know is just what I see. You haven't told me much of anything, no facts, no details, just that you were gonna be hit."

"Well, what happened back there—"

"Look, if you're trying to tell me the police are behind this, I'm not buying. Even *you* didn't think they were gonna pull that."

"You're not buying. Terrific. No, I wasn't looking for cops. Right. But at least I'm *learning.* You never learn. You get set up, it doesn't teach you anything; you get shot at, it doesn't mean anything to you. Meanwhile, we both get blown to hell."

"Maybe. Maybe not." He reached down, took her arm at the elbow, and pulled her up. For an instant, Mally wanted to scream all her reasons into his head. As if maybe by sheer volume she could penetrate his stubborn refusal to face facts. But then an icy calm came over her; both of their lives were out of their own control. Whoever was after them was deciding everything. There was nothing for either of them to do, nothing but curl up in a ball and brace for the impact. And when it was over, either they'd be dead or they'd still be alive. It was that simple. That absurdly simple.

"Let's go," he said. With controlled nonchalance, he took her hand in his. The grip was not friendly, simply practical.

"Look normal," he grunted.

"I *am* normal, Shockley."

Together they crossed the shallow patch of scrub that opened onto a quiet, residential street. A young boy on a bicycle rode past them, never giving a thought to the perfectly ordinary couple out for a leisurely late-aftemoon stroll, hand in hand.

CHAPTER 11

They passed an occasional parked car on the street, Ben glancing into each one. On a corner, behind a small, black topped parking lot, stood a small, unadorned taco stand. It was not busy; no one was visible behind the counter.

At the rear of the lot, secluded under a pair of trees, was a lone car with a large star on the door under the word "Sheriff." The driver was sunk low in the seat, his cap tilted forward over his eyes. Ben tugged firmly on Mally's hand, angling them toward the car. "Look like we got ourselves a ride," he said.

"That's a cop car, for chrissake!"

"Perfect."

Ben gave a quick glance up and down the street as they walked through the lot. Then he sprinted the last few yards to the blind side of the car.

The deputy was slouched behind the wheel, eating a taco. The barrel of Shockley's Magnum slid through the open window and came to rest a few inches from the scraggly sideburn that ran the length of his left ear.

The deputy froze.

"Do what I say, and it won't go off," Ben said quietly. "Now let's see those hands—nice and slow."

A fleck of shredded lettuce still clinging to his lower lip, the deputy raised his hands slowly above his head till his fingers touched the roof. His frightened eyes remained fixed on the windshield.

Ben nodded to Mally. "Get in."

She quickly climbed into the back seat and shut the door.

Ben immediately circled around the front of the car to the passenger side, the muzzle of his gun never shifting its bead from the deputy's face. He slipped into the front seat and slammed the door. "Go!"

The deputy tossed the remains of the taco out his open window, switched on the ignition, and eased out of the lot.

"Which way?" he said in a shaking voice.

"Left."

The deputy turned left. Left or right made no difference to Ben—he didn't know which way they should head—but giving a firm order did. A nervous man like this deputy would respond to somebody who seemed to know what he was doing.

Once they were on the road, the deputy seemed to relax a little, as if the familiar act of driving was somehow a buffer between him and the presence of danger—he wouldn't be shot so long as they wanted him to drive. "Don't get all jumpy now with that cannon, partner," he said. "I ain't no trouble. Ain't gonna *be* no trouble."

"Twenty of your buddies just tried to blow me to hell," Ben said icily. "They were trouble *but* trouble."

The deputy stole a quick glance at his captor. "You're two of them that was holed up in that cathouse, ain't you?"

"You already know about that?" Ben narrowed his eyes at him.

"Hell, every cop in this town knows about it."

"*What* do you know?"

The deputy shrugged. "Dispatcher said there was this hooker and four, maybe five men, armed and dangerous.

Said maybe they was gonna make bombs in there. Maybe they was terrorists of one kind or another. Half the units in the city must've tuned in."

Shockley exhaled a long breath, feeling Mally's harsh stare on the back of his head.

"Was you gonna make bombs?" the deputy asked.

"Yeah, and I put "em all in the cylinders of this gun."

"Okay, okay, just askin' friendly. That's what the dispatcher said, is all I know, that you was..."

Shockley reached into his pocket, pulled out his detective's shield, and flashed it in front of the deputy's eyes. "I don't know what half-ass story came over your radio, but there was just the two of us in that house. And I'm a cop."

The deputy, confident now that he was only a chauffeur, became more and more relaxed as he drove. He looked over at the shield, a faint snarl curling his lips. "Sheee-it, you think that little bit a tin proves anything? You mighta got it in a Cracker Jacks."

"You willing to stake your life on that?"

The deputy's hands gripped the wheel a little tighter. "Two fellas in a car said you shot at 'em. Made 'em crash. Put 'em in the hospital. Why would a cop do that?"

In the back seat, Mally's mind raced back over the wild chase in the ambulance, her firing of the unfamiliar gun, the terrible crash; and further back, the explosion, the torn body...

She thought she should have felt relief at the knowledge that she hadn't killed anyone, but she felt nothing except the fear and shock that had seized her during those moments.

She'd always abhorred violence. Even in her world where violence seemed always a threat, where johns or pimps could turn crazy, and working girls could, too; she had avoided it, avoided even acknowledging that it was around her.

But in the few hours since Shockley had claimed her from her cell, violence had taken over her whole life, drawn her into it, made her a participant. Violence had become her own perverse, surrealistic game, a game that admitted neither hope nor regret. It was a matter of sheer survival, like a trapped animal gnawing through its own leg to get free.

These things flashed through her mind even while the men kept talking.

"Do you understand what I'm telling you?" Ben's words hammered at the deputy. *"They* were shooting at *us!"*

"Well, that just ain't their story, is all I'm telling you. They say you was fleeing the scene of an accident, some car you runned into, and made it blow up. They say they was tailing you, just keepin' track of where you went, when you opened up at 'em, almost killed 'em—would've, too, if they had hit a wall instead of that plate glass window."

"They're full of shit."

The deputy nodded. "I'd say somebody is, that's for sure."

A city squad car pulled up and stopped at an intersection as they approached. The two men inside it waved.

"Wave back," Ben snapped.

The deputy stared straight ahead.

Ben jammed the Magnum into his side. "I said *wave!* Or this will cut you in two! Then we'll see if *they* believe this badge!"

Just as they were passing the stopped squad car, the deputy gave a quick wave. The squad car pulled across the intersection behind them, and disappeared.

Ben stuffed his shield back into his inside coat pocket and tried to pull his thoughts together. The dispatcher's voice crackled over the two-way radio, calling somebody else.

"You bein' a cop," the deputy said cautiously, "and sayin' you ain't done none of that stuff they say, maybe you wouldn't mind if I pick up the mic and tell 'em you're in the car here with me, and safe and all?"

"Don't touch it." Ben clicked off the radio and pulled the

gun from the deputy's holster. "Okay, buddy, what's your detail?"

"You're makin' it a whole lot worse, kidnappin' an officer of the law. You know that, don't you?"

"Just give me your detail, cowboy."

The deputy let out a small sign of defeat. "I got the west side shift—just cruise. Sundown, I turn in the car and hang up the hat."

"Well, you're gonna go a little out of your way today. Head for the border—Arizona."

"You tryin' to make Mexico? You ain't got a prayer in—"

"Arizona, I said. That's all you gotta worry about."

The deputy turned south at the next intersection. "They're gonna be wonderin' why I don't check in, you know."

"You'll have a great story for them, when you're finished with us."

"Suit yourself."

A few blocks later, the deputy turned a smiling, comradely face to Ben. "Tell you what—I'll make you a deal."

"No deals. Just drive."

"Now, hold on. Deals ain't nothin' bad. The whole world runs on deals, compromises, and—"

"And no sociology lectures."

"Now, listen, it's not gonna hurt you to hear me out, is it? I mean, if you're really a cop, let's us turn in this little clit here to the people what's been lookin' for her, and I'll see my way clear to forget the few little... uh... irregular liberties you've been takin'. Sound good? Reasonable, right?"

"You know who they are?"

"Huh?"

"The people who've been after her. How are you going to deliver her if you don't know who they are?"

"Well, I can't rightly say I know—"

"Look," Ben turned to face him, talking earnestly. "She

thinks somebody's after her ass, to keep her from leaving town, with me. Somebody's trying to kill her. Like those two in that car who shot at us. Like whoever bombed that other one—right, I said *bombed.* And then at that house, we were—"

"Hold it, Shockley!" Mally bolted forward in her seat.

"Jesus, man, you don't go spilling everything and angling for some kinda half-ass deal, when you don't even know who he might—"

"Cool it, Mally."

"Well, Christ! You're a cop, remember?"

"Shut up. You had your chance; now it's his turn. Okay, cowboy, throw me some names."

The deputy ran his tongue across his dry lips. "Well… Let's say for the minute your story's true—about them two dudes in the car shootin' at you first. If them dudes are examples, I'd say the folks huntin' her would have the initials M.O.B."

"I said *names"*

"What the hell, I didn't go to school with 'em."

"Then your deal stinks." Ben spun to face Mally. "God dammit, who the hell are you protecting?"

"I'm not protecting anybody!" Her voice was shrill, innocent.

"You *gotta* know more than you're telling! It's not a party game, Mally! They're already after you! It's not gonna get you in any deeper to tell me who they are!"

"I don't know, I don't know, I don't know!" She buried her face in her hands.

Ben faced the windshield and slumped down in his seat.

"Shit," he said flatly, his gun still steady in his hand.

The deputy smiled, then quickly straightened his mouth "Quite a fix you're in," he drawled. "How it looks, you're runnin' from the mob, and you got the cops on your ass, too. The good guys and the bad guys. Twixt a rock and a hard place, that's where you're at. And that badge you got to protect you, that's just what they're all gonna be aimin' at, ain't it? You ain't got a snowball's chance in hell. Nossir."

Ben wanted to bellow at him, roar his rage at the stupid reasoning, wanted to whip the asshole's head with his Magnum.

But he sat still and made no comment. He didn't have to; everything the man said was the truth. He was caught between two armies, occupying a no-man's-land whose boundaries were rapidly closing in on him. A duck in a shooting gallery, and all the customers were expert marksmen—and they were ready to stand there around the clock.

But there was damn little he could do about it. Run and hide, run and hide, keep moving toward his goal, little by little. His wits against all of theirs. And they knew him while he didn't know them.

One thing he had going for him—for as long as he could keep going. His life was on the line. Desperation, the primal will to survive, would help him. He would be a tough man to kill.

If he believed he'd have even an outside chance of convincing the Vegas police about what was happening, if he had had a chance to make them wait and listen before blowing him apart, he'd have taken it. But with the misinformation they were apparently being fed, there was no way they were going to believe him without a great deal of checking. And in the meantime, Mally would be out of his jurisdiction and even more vulnerable than she already was.

Why Blakelock hadn't confided the importance of the assignment to him was none of his business. Maybe Blakelock himself hadn't even known the ramifications. In any event, the assignment was to deliver a witness, and odds or no odds, that was what Ben Shockley was going to do.

Or, he reminded himself, almost chuckling at the appropriate cliché, he would die trying.

"So what do you say, Colonel?" The deputy was getting bolder all the time. "We can give her up. It don't have to be all bad. Let's the two of us get ourselves a little taste of that honey, then turn her ass in. Okay? What the hell, she's a pro, nobody'd pay attention if she said anything about—"

"Pull over." Ben had caught sight of a pay phone half a block ahead.

"What?" The deputy smiled. "We gonna do it?"

"Fuck you! Stop the car!"

They came to a half just beyond the phone booth.

"What're you fixin' to do?" The deputy's smile was gone, as was the confidence in his voice.

"Put the cuffs on her, one bracelet on her arm, the other on the roll bar."

The deputy took a quick glance at the Magnum pointed directly at his stomach, then reached into the back seat and did as he was told.

Shockley removed the keys from the ignition and dropped them into his coat pocket.

"Tough guys," Mally snarled as the cuffs clicked into place. "Big tin-star egomaniacs."

Ben ordered the deputy out and followed him away from the car.

Mally sat shacked in the back seat, twisting around as she watched the two men walk back to the phone booth. She tried to put herself in Shockley's place, not because she wanted to be sympathetic, but to try to see the priorities as he might see them. At least he wasn't lying to her, she was pretty sure about that. His back was to the wall—no doubt about that. But would he actually try to make a deal? If he did, she was as good as dead. Wouldn't he see that? Would he, after having come this far, actually sacrifice her to save his own ass?

He was the only one around patently not part of the forces out to get her. She didn't know who was behind this nightmare, but whoever it was certainly wouldn't think twice about dealing and then eliminating all the loose ends, including their sex-starved chauffeur.

And including Shockley himself. Would he be dumb enough to fall for it? For any kind of deal with those people? The trouble with cops, she cursed to herself, is that you never knew *where* the fuck their heads were.

She yanked fiercely on the handcuffs and succeeded only in bruising her wrist.

If Shockley was selling her out, so be it. Nothing she could do about it, under the present circumstances. He would get his, by and by. At least it would be an end to the madness. Or so she tried to tell herself, but she was only half convinced.

Now that she was faced with the possibility, giving up wasn't nearly as easy as she would have liked it to be.

She remembered that Shockley had asked her if there was anyone in town whom she could trust. Maybe the person he was talking to now, on the phone, was someone *he* could trust. One thing about Shockley, he stuck to his guns, literally and figuratively. Guy like that was likely to have a friend of similar attitude. Maybe it would be someone who could reach in and pluck them from the battle.

That dream, however unrealistic, was all she had left.

Her neck tiring from the awkward angle, she turned away from watching the phone booth and gave the seat-back in front of her a good kick.

She wondered if her life was being bartered away on the telephone.

Down the street, Shockley gripped the receiver tightly, in his left hand. The deputy was wedged in the booth with him, the barrel of the Magnum hard against his belly. Shockley waited for his call to go through.

. . .

Blakelock was occupied with a very interesting tape recording, and his intercom buzzed three times before he was aware of it.

Angry at the interruption, he snapped off the recorder and pushed the "Talk" button. "Yeah, what is it?"

His secretary's cool, efficient voice filtered through the tiny speaker. "Detective Ben Shockley on line five, Commander. Collect from Las Vegas. I already accepted charges."

Blakelock's finger slipped off the talk-back switch, and then his hand moved swiftly to the telephone, punching in line five as he snatched the receiver from its cradle. "Shockley!"

"Yessir." It was a poor connection, and Ben's voice sounded fiat and far away.

"Why the hell... where are you calling from?"

"I'm in a phone booth on the outskirts of Vegas."

"Why the hell aren't you—I thought you were going to the airport!"

"I was, sir, until the cathouse went up in flames."

"What?"

"Somebody set me up. Vegas cops had a bad read on what was going on. The mob's out to blow your witness, and somewhere along the line the Vegas police got the word that there were armed gunmen inside. The next thing I knew, they hit the place with everything but a fucking H-bomb."

"You got out... you... the witness... You're both okay?"

"Hell no, we're not okay. We're running for our lives. I think it's about time you leveled with me about Augustina Mally, if I may be so bold, sir."

"None of your concern."

"It is when somebody's turning our own people against me."

"Misunderstanding. Must have been. Damn fuck-up somewhere."

"I think it's worse than that, Commander."

"What? Where's your proof?"

"Proof? Against the *mob?* Come off it, *sir.* I've got a scorched ass, that's all the proof I need! I'm sitting in the middle of nowhere with a witness you told me was nothing to nobody, and the whole of the town's shooting at me, and I'm goddam *scared!* So bring us in. Alive. Sir."

Blakelock hesitated, then his words rumbled across the phone, firm, direct, comforting to Shockley. "Don't worry. We'll bring you in. Where and when?"

"The state line. Just before the river. One hour from now. Send me an escort. I'll make it that far. I'll be traveling in a sheriff's car. Do you copy?"

"Affirmative, Shockley. You'll have it... the escort. But I don't want any more screw-ups... not this time."

"That makes two of us, Commander."

Ben slammed down the receiver, and the dial tone hummed in Blakelock's ear. The commander thoughtfully replaced the receiver and swiveled his chair back to face the tape recorder.

The reels spun in rewind, then jerked to a stop. Pressing a finger on the center switch, he leaned back and listened.

The first voice he heard was that of John Feyderspiel, a prosecuting attorney with the best conviction record in the D.A.'s office.

"I ask you now under penalty of perjury, Mr DeLucca, whether to your knowledge there are any witnesses who can corroborate what you have told the jury."

There was a pause on the tape, then a reply from a man obviously intimidated, scared, shaking.

"Well, yessir, maybe. One, sir. One that I can think of..."

CHAPTER 12

Shockley backed the deputy out of the phone booth by jabbing him in the belly with the Magnum, and they quickly covered the short distance back to the parked cruiser. The two men settled into their seats, and slammed the doors shut.

Ben fished out the handcuff keys and tossed them in the deputy's lap. "Take 'em off."

"I kinda like her better all trussed up, don't you?"

"If I have to ask you again, you're gonna be the one hanging from that roll bar."

"Okay, Colonel, don't get yourself all het up."

Mally stared past the deputy while he unfastened the bracelets. She felt his eyes on her breasts and smelled the strong odor of taco that clung to his breath.

When he was finished, he handed the paraphernalia to Ben and accepted the car keys in return.

"Now, take us to the state line," Ben said.

The deputy switched on the ignition, blipped the accelerator once, then turned to face him. "Listen, Colonel, now I heard some of that stuff on the phone, and I guess you really are a cop. So you know I got to call in at quittin' time—which it is now."

Ben knew the absence of the routine call would

generate immediate suspicion—if there wasn't suspicion already, since the deputy hadn't checked in from time to time.

"Okay, go ahead. Tell them you need the car another hour. Tell them you been out of the car for a while, some kind of personal emergency. Tell them your mother-in-law was hit by a truck. Tell them your aunt came down with typhoid. Tell them anything, but make believers out of them. If you don't, I'll make a believer out of *you* before you can say ten-four."

"I'll try. But that's a tall order. I ain't used to—"

"You're just the man to carry it out," Shockley said calmly. "You've got one chance to do it right."

"Yeah. Jesus. Okay."

The deputy clicked on the radio, removed the mic from the dashboard, and called in. He told them his mother-in-law was hit by a truck—not serious enough for an ambulance, that's why he hadn't called for one, and no need for another police car, since he was already there, but he'd been tied up for a while, kind of upset…

The first minutes of darkness encircled them as they glided along the highway. The closer they got to the state line, the spottier the tense conversation became. The three riders brooded.

Glancing in the rear-view mirror, the deputy grinned at Mally's dimly lit reflection. "Mind if I ask you a question, lady?"

She made no reply, but looked out of the side window.

"How many times you spread your legs in a month?"

"Cowboy," Ben said, "just keep driving. She's no business of yours."

"Aw, now…" The deputy smiled. He seemed to grow less fearful of Shockley as they drove, as if Shockley didn't seem the type that would shoot a fellow officer, not for just talking.

"Hey, now," he went on, "I got me a chance to learn something, Colonel. Ain't often a guy like me gets a chance like this. Long's I gotta chauffeur the little whore, you don't mind if a country boy like me picks up a little education, do you?" He cackled lightly. "You know, I got this here buddy, good friend of mine. He had the idea one time we'd open a string of whorehouses and advertise 'em like fried chicken places —'finger-lickin' good!" His cackle was louder.

He leered at Mally in the mirror, and she met his gaze with a cold stare.

"How's it work with your kind?" he continued. "You go to a special school to learn how to do all that special stuff?"

"As a matter of fact," she said flatly, "I have a college degree. Bachelor of Arts."

"Bachelor! Haw! Bet you do more married men than bachelors!" He grinned over at Shockley. "But no kiddin', you went to college? That where you learned to get ahead? And *give* head?" He belched laughter.

"Will you shut up?" Shockley didn't like the look on the deputy's face. And somehow, talk like that always made him uncomfortable in front of women, even a hooker.

"Say, now," the deputy grinned at him, "you comin' to her rescue, Colonel? Bet you had ideas of gettin' a little gash for yourself, huh? Maybe you already tasted it. Nothin' like a slice of damp, is there?"

Shockley's jaw tightened with anger as the deputy gave him a conspiratorial wink. "Naw, we ain't no different, you and me. After the same thing. You can't fool ol' Deke. I seen you zippin' your fly."

Ben jammed the Magnum into the man's side. "Shut the fuck up! Starting now!"

This time the deputy looked down at the gun with a snicker of amusement. "You gonna kill a fellow officer,

Colonel? What'll you tell 'em back home? That I was insultin' your own private whore? Heh-heh."

It was clear he knew that Shockley wouldn't pull the trigger.

Disgusted with himself for allowing the conversation to develop, disgusted with the whole damn situation and everything that had led up to it, disgusted with his inability to get it under control, Ben turned away and glared through the windshield at the thin stripe of white line illuminated by the car's advancing headlights. He hoped it wouldn't take long to reach the state line; he was not sure he could go on controlling himself.

"Well, now"—the deputy's eyes were on the mirror again—"how do you like that, lady?" His voice was thick. "Looks like you done lost your hero-boy. Looks like he ain't gonna defend your *honor!*

"Don't worry yourself, Deke-boy," Mally said calmly. "I can take care of myself."

"Ho-ho, I'll bet you can. I'll bet you can handle yourself just fine. I'll bet you earn every little penny. So let's just you and me have us a little talk, okay? I just *love* to talk, *love* to get to know all about people, what makes 'em tick, how they do their jobs."

"You've got a real thirst for knowledge, don't you?"

"Oh, absolutely."

"Watch the fuck where you're going!" Ben grabbed the wheel and whipped it half a turn to keep them out of a drainage ditch.

"Sure thing, sure thing." The deputy nodded, smiling. "I got her. Maybe you'd like to drive, though. Maybe I should just crawl in the back and take me a little nap—it's past my duty, you know."

"Drive, turkey."

The deputy looked back into the mirror. "Now tell me,

lady, you ever go down on another girl? Ever had it done to you?" He chuckled wetly. "Whores don't ball just guys, do they? I mean, you'll do it with anybody's got the cash, right? And I heard where whores sometimes actually *prefer* to have another girl do it to them. How 'bout that? So much stuff I heard. Glad to get a chance to chat with you about it. Heh-heh."

Smoothly, her hands steady, not the slightest line of emotion on her face, Mally lit a cigarette. She exhaled the first deep drag from calm, untroubled lips, right at the deputy's head.

He coughed lightly and shook his head as the cloud enveloped him. Then he smiled into the mirror, speaking more rapidly. "I'll bet you do all those things, don't you? Bet I'd like to watch you, too. You can lay odds on that. Yes, ma'am. I could really dig watchin'—them pretty little melons all pink and tight; that little ass a-humpin' and a-twistin'; them long legs all jacked up an' juicy-like; hands grabbin' everywhere." He licked his lips. "I'll bet it don't take much to get your pussy all wet and hot-to-trot, now, does it? I mean, come on, talk to me. I really want to know. What's it like exactly, bein' a *whore?*'

"Actually"—her reply came back without hesitation, and she blew a smoke ring toward the roof—"I always thought it was rather like being a cop."

The deputy grunted involuntarily, then forced a harsh laugh.

"Surprised, Deke-boy?" she went on, studying the back of his head. "I don't see why. What I do for a living isn't much different from your being on the take at two dozen bars in downtown Vegas. Or accepting money from the senator each time you peel his kid's Cadillac off a telephone pole. Or looking the other way when a big shot gets five-oh-two'd, then strong-arming Chicanos in the barrio on Saturday night to get your rocks off. Or busting kids for smoking grass, then taking kickbacks from the dealers. And what about all those times when you bust a skag-pusher, skim the haul when you've made the collar, then sell what you skim to your dope-addict buddies on the force?"

She leaned back and looked at his eyes in the mirror. "Any of that sound familiar, *officer?*"

The deputy squirmed uncomfortably in his seat. "She's sure on to all our tricks, ain't she, Colonel?" He jutted an elbow toward Shockley. "She must be givin' it to quite a few cops, too, 'cause she's sure got it down." He smiled stiffly.

"Why certainly. Deke-boy." Mally's tone was light and even. "As I see it, the only difference between you and me is that after I finish work I take a long, hot bath and I'm clean as the day I was born. But a cop like you—when the sheriff whistles, you squat. And when you pull your little extra-duty numbers, he likes you, because he's doing it, too. He treats you like the filthy slave you are. And what he does to you rots your mind. And no amount of water on earth can make you clean again. Because the dirt is all inside, coating your brain and belly and balls like scum. Hmmm?"

"Hey," the deputy snarled at Shockley, "you gonna sit there and take that shit from a prisoner?"

"You're the one who asked her to talk," Shockley said, not bothering to look at him. "And I don't believe she's talking to me, right?"

"Well, what kinda—"

"I know you don't like women like me," Mally continued in the soothing tones of a mother patiently informing her child. "We seem a bit aggressive. We frighten you. We threaten your manhood. You're afraid you couldn't get it up, with someone like me. But that's because you've got scum on your brain and the only way you'll ever clean it out is to make a nice, neat hole. With a bullet."

She paused, smiling as she watched the cords of the deputy's neck pulse with anger.

"By the way," she cooed, leaning forward toward his reddened ear, "does your wife know you masturbate?"

CHAPTER 13

An involuntary spasm made the deputy's foot slam on the brakes, locking them and sending the car into a screeching fishtail over the center line and into the path of an oncoming trailer truck.

The deputy wrestled for control of the runaway car, whipping the wheel back and forth, landing them finally on the soft shoulder of the road just as the lights of the truck flashed by. The sound of the truck's blaring air horn faded away.

The car skidded and jolted to a stop.

They had barely avoided disaster. But for the deputy, the shock of the near miss was overshadowed by the burning truth of Mally's insults.

He lunged at Ben, grasping for the Magnum with the savage hysteria of a jilted lover.

The two men grappled for the weapon. Ben wrestled it free and cracked the butt sharply against the side of the deputy's head.

The next sound in the car was the crisp click of the hammer being levered back by Shockley's thumb.

His breath coming in hollow bursts, the deputy gazed dumbly at him, his eyes fiery and wet.

"You've had your chat," Ben said evenly. "Now drive."

Blood trickled steadily from the deputy's lacerated scalp, rounding his ear and dripping onto his shoulder. He spun the wheel viciously, sending the car sliding back onto the highway, his choke-hold on the wheel turning the knuckles of his hands as white as his ashen face.

Ben glanced quickly back at Mally, and in the brief second that their eyes met and held, a spark of mutual recognition passed between them.

The recognition was of the fact that they had got to know each other a lot better, all of a sudden. Then they settled back in their seats and let the hum of the tires against the road lull them into a limbo of fragile peace.

"Shockley?" Mally's quiet voice pierced the silence.

"Yeah?" he answered, without looking back.

"What's going to happen at the border?"

"We're picking up an escort."

"Who?"

"Cops. Out-of-state cops. Arizona."

"How do you know?" she asked, still softly.

"Because that's what I asked for. That's what I'll get."

"Oh." She hesitated, then continued, hoping that her voice carried no trace of hostility or accusation. "Did you call the same person you telephoned from the house?"

Ben turned slowly to face her. "What are you trying to say?"

"Oh, well..." She looked at her lap and bit her lip, wondering how to put it so he would let her say it all, before his loyalties would force him to cut her off. "It's just that, okay, it's like this. Somebody's trying to kill me. Okay. And since you're along, you're a target, too. Okay, so maybe the car that blew up, the two men who shot at us, maybe that all came from down under. But at the house, Ben, those were *policemen* outside. Okay? Somehow they got the wrong message. There's a possibility it was a legitimate mistake, garbled radio call or something. But what if it wasn't?"

She watched his eyes, saw him blink.

"What if somebody deliberately misinformed them? Who could it have been? Who would have given them the wrong message? Where did it come from?"

Ben turned to face front. He watched the hour hand on the dashboard clock jerk ahead a fraction of an inch.

"You're not telling me anything I haven't thought of already," he said at last. "But it wasn't my guys. Not my own department. I know the place. If there was a tie-in with the police—and I'm a big enough boy to know those things happen—then the hook-up was in Vegas. That's the only thing that makes sense. Vegas is where everything was happening, including the bomb and the shooting and the mob or whatever. It would be the Vegas P.D."

"You're probably right." Mally studied her hands. "But let's say, just say, there's a chance you're wrong. Just one. One chance in a thousand." She paused, a bit fearful of going on, and curled her toes to absorb her tension. "The state line's a lonely place to find out."

"You gonna take that kind of shit?" The deputy hadn't spoken since he took Shockley's blow. Now he muttered bitterly. "You hear what that bitch is sayin', 'bout your own men?"

Ben shot a look at Mally, then turned to the deputy. "How far to the line?"

"Another five, six miles. Five minutes. You don't honestly believe that crap she's handing out, do you?" He seemed honestly affronted.

Ben's eyes dropped to the speedometer. The slender red needle was holding steady at sixty; the digits that marked the tenths of miles rolled steadily over.

. . .

Arriving at the border from the opposite direction, a five-car convoy snaked through the darkness and came to rest on the sandy shoulder of the highway.

The driver of the lead car snatched a radio mic from its bracket and pressed the talk-back switch. His passenger sat immobile, a shotgun propped between his knees.

"Hunt Master relay, this is Red Fox One. Do you copy?"

The reply filtered through the radio. "We read you, Red Fox One."

"All vehicles at state line. Parked and ready. Rabbit should arrive any minute now, if he maintains his schedule."

"We copy, Red Fox One. Make sure you don't cross the line."

"Got it. Ten-four."

"Ten-four, Red Fox One. Will relay to Hunt Master."

The driver replaced the mic, then extinguished the car's headlights.

One by one, as if it were some well-rehearsed drill, the lights on the other four cars followed the lead until only their barely noticeable silhouettes were visible under the silver crescent of moon.

"State line's just beyond that rise up ahead," the deputy said grumpily. Then he scowled. "Good thing you're lightin' outta here, Colonel. I ever see your ass again, I'll cut off your pecker and shove it down your gullet."

Shockley leaned slowly toward him, smiling. "I think you'll be keeping your hands to yourself."

The deputy stared straight ahead, his lips working wordlessly.

"Shockley?" The plea behind Mally's voice was unmistakable.

"I hear what you're saying," he answered.

The sheriff's car began to climb the long rise.

"I may be wrong," Mally said. "But what if I'm right?"

"I said I heard you." Ben continued to stare ahead. The deputy pressed down harder on the accelerator, pushing the car faster toward the top of the incline. The crest of the hill began to take shape in the darkness.

"Pull over," Ben ordered.

"Huh?"

"Stop the fucking car!"

"Like hell." The deputy's foot whomped the accelerator to the floor causing, the car to leap ahead. Shockley rammed the barrel of the Magnum deep into the man's side.

Emitting a sharp whistle of breath and a stifled grunt of pain, the deputy backed his foot off, and the car slowed.

Mally closed her eyes in relief.

They pulled off the road just before the top of the rise.

Shockley jumped out of the car and opened the rear door for Mally, his movements never once obstructing the steady aim he held on the deputy.

She stood next to Ben as he slammed the back door and tossed the deputy's gun to the ground. "You go ahead and meet them," he told the deputy. "I'll leave your gun right here. You can come back and get it."

"You damn well bet I will. And I won't be alone, neither. You're gonna have some fast talking to do, Colonel. Those fellas waiting on you are gonna wonder why you bailed out. I'm gonna tell 'em you chose sides—chose sides against the law. Got yourself a little nookie and chose the side against your own."

Ben slammed the passenger door shut. The car jumped away as the tires bit into the sand.

Mally started to say thanks, but Ben grabbed her roughly by the arm and led her on a course parallel to the highway and up the remaining section of the hillside to the crest.

He was playing a hunch—her hunch. But he was hedging.

If she turned out to be wrong, he wanted to be close

enough to explain himself to the Arizona cops before the deputy got his chance to run his mouth in revenge.

"Get down," Ben told Mally. They dropped to the ground at the top of the hill, chins above the sparse grass, and watched the tail lights of the sheriff's car as it moved steadily over the crest and down toward the state line.

The five-car convoy waited in the darkness.

"Car coming," the man with the shotgun said to the lead driver.

"I can see it."

The headlights were a mile away. The five engines of the convoy idled.

"Think it's the rabbit?"

"Don't know."

A camping van passed the convoy, headed toward Nevada. Half a minute later, its headlights briefly illuminated the sheriff's car coming toward it.

"It's him, all right," the driver of the convoy's lead car said.

"Call in."

His passenger took the mic. "Red Fox One to all units. Rabbit approaching."

"Copy, Red Fox One. We see him," radioed the last car in line.

The deputy passed a sign that said, "Welcome to Arizona: Grand Canyon State." He strained his eyes for signs of Shockley's escort and shook his head. He had expected to see some kind of roadblock or something—flares, something official.

But there was nothing. Maybe the whole thing was a ruse —the phone call, all the talk—just to allow them to get to the border and get Shockley over it, into Arizona and out of the jurisdiction where he could be arrested.

The deputy considered turning back. "Cocksuckers are back there laughin' at me," he muttered aloud. "I could go back right now and take 'em—they haven't got outta Nevada yet, the bastards."

But he didn't even have a gun. And by the time he called in for assistance, and cars could get here, the bastard-asshole-cocksuckers would be long gone.

The deputy decided he'd drive a little farther.

He thought about Mally and all the things he'd like to do to her. Before he cut off her tits.

Then he saw a set of headlights flash at him, a few hundred yards ahead.

Back on the crest of the hill, Ben saw the flash of the headlights, too. "Come on, they're meeting him. Let's start down there. We won't have much time."

He and Mally started trotting down the hill, toward the state line.

The men of the convoy saw the lights of the deputy's car blink in reply. Now only the drivers were left in the cars, revving the engines slightly in a rhythmic rise and fall.

The rest of the men, all in civilian clothes, were out beside the cars, crouching, settling the stocks of their shotguns against their shoulders.

The command burst from the convoy radios: "Take him."

Simultaneously, the headlights of all five cars lit up on high beam.

The deputy was just about to move his foot to the brake when the powerful beams blazed into his eyes. He raised his left arm as a shield against the lights. The sound of the shotgun blasts reached him a split second after the first wall of ammunition tore into his car.

For an instant his eyes bulged with horrified surprise, and in that same instant his windshield exploded and a thousand tiny slugs ripped through.

His world was suddenly a vicious, twisting amalgam of shattering glass and ruptured metal as the searing fusillade made a sieve of his vehicle.

Blood spurted from his face, neck and chest. He sagged down into his seat as the pellets tore him apart.

The gunfire ceased abruptly. The madly swerving sheriff's car jounced across the rugged desert terrain, the flapping of its hood and trunk lid giving it the ungainly appearance of a crippled bird desperately seeking the air. Finally it came to rest in a brittle clump of tumbleweed, a steaming hulk.

CHAPTER 14

At the sound of gunfire, Ben and Mally, who had been racing down the hill, flopped to the ground and buried their faces in the dirt, not knowing where the bullets were coming from and where they would hit.

When the firing stopped, they looked quickly up. They saw the five ambush cars snake into a synchronous u-turn and head back along the highway. As their lights swung over each other in the turn, Ben could see that the cars were unmarked.

Slowly he rose to his feet. The cool night breeze skimmed over the crest of the hill and down it, ruffling his hair. He started back up the hill.

Mally's eyes followed him. Then she got up and climbed, too.

Ben stood at the crest, silhouetted by the moon, staring down at the ruined sheriff's car. Mally reached his side and looked from him to the car and back. Then Ben turned and walked down the hill. Away from the scene. Away from the highway. Into the night.

Mally watched him descend. A dumb cop, she thought, not really meaning it. A stubborn, single-minded fool. He would have walked right into that ambush himself, given a few more minutes. And taken her with him.

But he had not—by whatever grace of God. He might have, but he hadn't. Because he had listened to her. He had got them out of the car and kept them alive. He had shown at least that much caution, that much regard for her suspicions—enough to keep them alive.

And try as she might to convince herself otherwise, she knew that they were inextricably united by a common circumstance; they were both alone—totally, frighteningly alone, except for each other. And however close he seemed determined to bring them to disaster, one way or another he was able to elude it. Or she was.

They needed each other to stay alive.

She brushed the sand from her clothes and hurried down the hill to catch up with him.

Their shelter for the night was the lee of a huge boulder at the base of a rock-strewn mountain.

Shockley hunched over a meager fire, the undulating light from the flames playing across the shadows and lines that streaked his gaunt and tired face.

Mally had been huddled against the uneven wall of rock, but her need for warmth eventually drew her toward the fire.

They had not spoken since the violent ambush of the deputy. Now, hesitantly, she reached out and touched his shoulder. She felt him flinch. She said, "If it's any consolation—"

"What?"

She withdrew her hand. "Nothing."

"Good. Then shut up."

She knelt close to the small flames, her defenses returning as the heat seeped into her body. "I never saw a cop feeling sorry for himself before. Mind if I watch?"

She was the embodiment of all that had happened to him in the last thirty-six hours, and he hated the last thirty-six hours. "For two cents and a stick of gum I'd beat the shit out of you." He didn't look at her.

"Whatever gets you off, butch."

"And when I'm through, where do I leave my twenty bucks?"

A john is a john is a john, she thought bitterly, whether he's in a cave or a hundred-dollar hotel suite. "I don't want your money, Shockley. I love you for your *mind.*'

His open right hand flew up in a blur, catching her hard across the face with a whip-like slap that cracked against the stillness of the night and sent her reeling sideways.

She recovered instantly, and the next thing Shockley felt was the wind rushing out of him and pain rushing in—the toe of her shoe had caught him squarely in the crotch.

Doubled up with agony, he slumped against the boulder, moaning.

She took a cigarette from her purse and lit it. "Sorry about that," she said through a mouthful of smoke. "I just wanted to jog your thinking."

He cursed quietly as he looked at the ground, waiting for the pain to subside. His mind sifted briskly through a dozen alternatives for avenging what Mally had done to him—not just the kick, but everything.

Mally stood with legs apart and hands on hips, looking at him with a mixture of pity and disdain. "You're a loser, Shockley. I'm splitting."

She flung her purse over her shoulder and stalked off, quietly fading into the darkness. She was half a dozen steps away when she heard the Magnum's firing mechanism click into readiness. She stopped, but did not turn around. "How about it, Shockley? You gonna shoot an unarmed woman in the back? Go ahead. Easy way to get your *job* over with. But how'll it look on your stinking record?"

Ben slowly straightened up. The pain had finally eased enough to allow him to speak evenly. "You don't stand a chance, *period*! On my own, I do okay. I've always managed on my own."

"Oh, really? Who kept that deputy off your ass?"

"Don't take any bows, buster. *You* brought that sick pig into this. And if it wasn't for me, you'd have let him drive us right into those guns."

"If it wasn't for you, there wouldn't *be* any goddam guns! It's *you* they're trying to kill, remember?"

"It's both of us, you stupid bastard! Don't you see that yet? Just why the hell do you think you drew this assignment?"

"I'm here because I get the job done."

She whirled to face him, her fists clenched, her eyes flickering in the firelight. "They don't *want* the job done! They sent you because you're a bum! If they waste you, nobody—not a fucking soul—is going to give a rat's ass! You're a nobody, Shockley. A nothing. You're just a faded number on a rusty badge, and you've been set up by your own people to take the fall with me! Wake up, for chrissake! At least that way, when the bullets hit you, you'll know where they came from!"

She turned and walked away into the darkness.

He could have shot her, of course. He could have made her pay for every single word she'd hit him with, every pain she'd caused him since the beginning. Instead, he lowered the gun and stuck it under his belt.

Everything she'd said was the truth. He was the most expendable man in the precinct, the grinder who had plodded along for all those years *getting the job done.*

Except that his diligence had been his own undoing, his loyalty had been the ultimate proof of his uselessness. And so they'd sent him out to be killed. Somebody had. They'd written him off—and Mally, too—like so much excess baggage. All they were concerned about was keeping their desks clean and their ambitions well-oiled.

And that, he told himself bluntly, was why he was sitting alone in the middle of the goddam desert. Really alone—the sound of Mally's footsteps was gone.

"Hey!" he called out. "Watch out for the sidewinders!"

There was a silence, then: "What?"

Ben managed a half-smile. "Sidewinders. Rattlesnake. They only come out after dark."

Another silence. "Horse shit."

"Okay, don't believe me. But they're drawn by body heat. You'll never see them till they strike."

He waited, listening for her reply.

For thirty seconds he heard nothing. Then there was the sound of her feet shuffling along the sand, and soon she came into the light of the fire.

"I'll leave in the morning," she said sharply.

"Sure."

"I will, dammit. And I'll make it, too. You'll see."

She curled up on the sand, her back to him, her head resting on her outstretched arm. And now that she'd made the decision to stay the night, she was glad to let the exhaustion wash across her body.

Shockley looked at her, envying her relaxation, and the bitterness and anger surged through him again.

He said, "I guess if you were still in Vegas, you'd just be going to work about now, huh?"

She sighed. "You've been hanging around that deputy too much, Shockley. Why don't you polish your badge? It's all you've got left."

He turned to stare into the fire, watching the sparks drift upward and swirl away, feeling the heat against his cheek bones. Almost unconsciously, he withdrew his wallet and flipped it open. The badge glowed dully in the light from the flames.

Whether it was the patrolman's badge he had once displayed on his uniform, or the detective's shield that he now held, the entire sum of his adult life had been spent in the service of that insignia. For him, at least in the beginning, it had been the difference between living and merely existing.

And even when his dreams had been smoothed and dulled by routine, even then he'd felt he had a purpose, a reason for getting up in the morning and doing his job. And what had it got him? A seat by the fire with a whore who was marked for the kill.

"Miserable bitch." He spoke the words to the flames.

"Welcome to the ranks of the disenchanted." Mally's voice was already thick with drowsiness.

"Shut up and go to sleep."

"Yes, Daddy."

"Cunt."

"Your word-selection reveals you, friend." She stretched her legs luxuriously, then curled back up into a tight ball of warmth. "I'm a counter-puncher, Shockley," she yawned. "If you can't go the distance, stay out of the ring."

Weariness was flooding through him. He no longer had the spirit to top her; she'd never let him have the last word. Anyway, there was no last word to this kind of shit.

He closed his wallet and replaced it in his pocket. He wanted to shut out the world, to lose himself in sleep.

To get drunk—that was what he wanted. But though his body ached with fatigue, his mind was alive with memories of the recent past and forebodings of the hours yet to come.

And every thought told him he'd been dead since the moment he'd laid eyes on Augustina Mally.

Mally dreamed about snakes. Snakes were chasing her.

When she ran from them, she got warm, and they

pursued her all the more, more and more of them. When she stopped, her body cooled, and the snakes would stop surrounding her, wriggling and arching and flicking their forked tongues, but not touching her.

So her dilemma was that to run from the serpents meant to be forever pursued, but to stop meant to be forever surrounded by the ugly, slithering creatures.

And in her dream, she dared not sleep. She could not trust the snakes to be true to their natures; she could not trust her body to stay cool enough.

At last, she grew too tired of running and stopping to watch them. She could not keep herself from lying down.

She lay down and heard the snakes rustling around her.

From somewhere came human hands. She thought they might lift her up and away from her predicament. But they didn't. The human hands packed her in ice, covered her completely in a shimmering castle of it. And there she lay, saved from the snakes by being frozen to death.

Shockley did not sleep. He refused to give in to it. Partly he didn't trust Mally and couldn't risk her slipping away during the night. Partly he felt the need to reassert his own strength, his own willpower, over something. Over himself.

So he willed himself to stay awake.

But mostly he needed to think. He needed to form a plan, a design for the next step, and the next, to get them out of this.

The circumstances of the moment provided no raw stuff for a plan. They were somewhere in the desert, by definition a forsaken territory, how far from or near to civilization or danger he did not know. He couldn't even pick a direction to go in.

They had walked miles from the highway. They could walk the same miles back to it. But he dared not use a road, because their pursuers might well be prowling the entire route. Pursuers were now friend and foe alike, cops and robbers, indistinguishable.

He could deal with the idea of being hunted by the mob. He could not quite handle the notion of being hunted by the police. Yet somewhere between his own P.D. and himself, somebody had turned the cops on him. Who? He could figure out who if he just knew why.

He had few friends, but as far as he knew he had no particular enemies, either. No more than any cop who'd spent his years getting people locked up. You never knew about people you put away, people whose action you busted, whose freedom you erased. Crooks you sent to jail were always a threat when they got out. Their craving for vengeance could be all-consuming and endless.

That's why cops were so adamant about carrying guns while off duty; that's why retirement was in some ways such a myth, unless you moved away.

But nobody he'd ever busted could have such influence over the police.

He was not political, and so wasn't a threat to any politicians who might have sway over the police.

Someone in the department? No. He'd kept his nose clean, caused no trouble. He'd concentrated on his assigned cases, one by one, and solved them. He was not ambitious. He was no threat to anyone within the department.

He wasn't notorious in any way. He was a low-key, almost invisible, cop. He was, in all ways he could think of, a neutral, except when he was after somebody's ass to solve a case.

For all his lack of charisma, though, he was good, in the way that other cops recognize. He was efficient, thorough, and—as Josie often said—dogged as a bulldog. He focused his efforts intensely on each case, almost to the total exclusion of anything else that might be going on around him.

He got the job done.

The idea of somebody wanting to keep a witness from

testifying was nothing new. It was common, in fact. And so it was no shock that somebody might want to keep Mally off the stand. And it was not the first time he'd had to protect a witness from mortal harm.

But this was the first time he'd had to protect a witness for a trial in which he had no involvement at all, a trial that wasn't his own case.

That puzzled him, as it had from the beginning. But it just hadn't seemed important enough to worry about. Not before, anyway. If someone wanted to stop a witness from testifying, it stood to reason that they might also want to stop whatever cop had made the case. If it was an inside job, and you wanted to set up the cop *and* the witness, the logical thing, in a situation like this one, would be to send the cop to get the witness, and hit them both together, clean and quick.

That's why he couldn't figure this one. His participation had to be accidental. Somebody wanted Mally, and he just happened to be the one charged with protecting her and bringing her in. But somehow that didn't wash. Cops were involved, at some level. Because somewhere between him and Commander Blakelock, somebody stepped in and got him set up.

And that made no sense. Why him?

Ben knelt down. Writing in the sand with his finger, he made a list about himself:

1. Efficient
2. Neutral
3. Bulldog
4. Experienced (15 yrs)
5. Honest
6. Not Ambitious

He looked at the list and shook his head. There was no clue here as to why he would be set up. In fact, he felt a little embarrassed at listing so many positive qualities—he was glad he hadn't added "Brave, Clean and Reverent." Was there anything else? Anything Josie might add? Or anybody else? Only Mally. He shook his head again. But then he added to the list:

7. Blind

Nonsense. Whatever Mally thought was beside the point. *She* wasn't setting him up. And anyway, she was wrong.

However blind he might seem in the beginning, he always saw the facts and the truth eventually. Always.

He smoothed over the last point with his hand, erasing it.

Ben got up and stretched. He walked slowly around the side of the boulder and stood looking up at the stars in the clear desert sky. He took deep breaths of the clean air.

He leaned back against the boulder and took a cigarette from his shirt pocket and lit it, watching the embers glow orange in the dark.

Okay. Look at it another way. Backwards.

If he were the one putting out the hit order, why would he set up Ben Shockley?

He felt more comfortable going at it this way. Rather than just analyzing his own defensive position, he was doping out the mind of the perpetrator. Just as he would in an ordinary case.

Okay. The strengths and weaknesses of Ben Shockley would be the key. His strengths would be how he could hurt you. His weaknesses would suggest ways you could set him up.

Essentially, Ben Shockley's strengths were that he was efficient, experienced, tenacious, and honest.

His weaknesses were—what? Is not being ambitious a weakness?

Blindness would be a weakness.

Ben took a deep drag on his cigarette. Okay, he would take a look at blindness, along with lack of ambition.

He forced himself to focus on the cops. He had to admit that cops who knew him well would recognize that his lack of ambition contributed to a certain blindness in small ways.

It was true that he had an inability to grasp particular signs quickly. Even Josie recognized that; Josie often smelled danger before Ben did. And Mally had recognized it, too, in this case. And within the department, it was his lack of ambition that kept him from bothering to notice the nuances of schemes by which more ambitious cops plotted their rise to power.

So if some cops were plotting against him in relation to their reach for power, they could capitalize on the fact that he probably wouldn't be aware of their ambitions, however unholy, and would therefore be a good, blind, unsuspecting target for a quick, well-planned hit.

But why would Ben Shockley be a threat to any power-hungry cops? He didn't give a shit who ran the detective division or the bomb squad or the tactical force or undercover operations or various precincts or anything. He didn't even care who the chief was.

Just so long as it was a half-way decent department, reasonably free of corruption. The only time Ben Shockley would become a threat was if somebody wanted to take it all, and subvert it, maybe turn it over to organized—

Yes, there was a point at which Ben Shockley would become a threat. At the point at which his own P.D. was being sold out, and thereby the city with it, Ben Shockley would become a very serious threat indeed. Because he could not be bought. And he didn't give a shit who was doing the selling; whoever it was, Ben Shockley would be after his ass.

And he would use every bit of smarts he had acquired in fifteen years, and he would be efficient, and he wouldn't care where the chips fell, because he wasn't after anything for himself. He would be after the ass of anybody trying to sell out Ben Shockley's P.D. He would be tenacious; he would get the job done.

And everybody in the whole department knew that much about Ben Shockley. But the very notion of such a plot was mind-boggling. It was impossible, nonsense.

Unless he was every bit as blind as Mally said.

And unless she knew something more than she was telling.

Ben watched the first streaks of dawn define the horizon, thinking that he would have been much better off if he'd got a few hours sleep, instead of all this idle, childish pondering of imponderables.

Today would not be easy. But they couldn't stay in the desert.

CHAPTER 15

The light of the new morning gradually warmed the desert floor.

Mally stretched and shivered. The refreshment of the night's sleep was offset by a dull ache in the small of her back and a cold stiffness in all her muscles. Opening her eyes, she tried to recall her dreams—a habit with her, to give her otherwise disjoined life some continuity. Thinking about her dreams on the mornings after—knowing them, analyzing them, recognizing the themes—gave her a sense of her own complexity and substance and worth.

But this morning she couldn't call back her dreams. For seconds she was blank. Then the harsh and sinister reality came to her, and instead of her dreams, it was where she was and how she came to be there that she recalled.

For a moment she felt hunger, then fear—both basic animal-survival reactions, and both appropriate. She hadn't eaten in two days, two days during which they had barely escaped being killed in what seemed like a dozen attempts on their lives. She felt alone. Raising herself to her knees, she looked around and was glad to see that Shockley was still there.

His back to her, he was motionless in front of the cold

ashes of the fire, his eyes fixed on the copy of Mally's subpoena.

"Shockley?" She wanted communication, a response of any kind. "Ben?"

He sat staring at the document. She rose and walked slowly over to him, wrapping her arms around herself and rubbing with her hands to restore warmth. She stood looking down at him. "What's that writing, there in the sand?"

He quickly obliterated it with his hand, without speaking. "It had numbers," she said. "Did it have anything to do with me, with us? About our—"

"Who's DeLucca?" he asked quietly, without looking up.

"What?"

"DeLucca. Angelo DeLucca. He's the defendant in the trial—the trial I'm taking you back for. Angelo DeLucca, also known as 'Little Angel.'"

She rubbed her eyes. "You been sitting there all night? Didn't you get any sleep at all?"

He folded the subpoena and stuffed it back in his pocket. Then he looked up at her, his face a haggard mask of fatigue. "You're supposed to be a witness, either for him or against him. Who is he?"

Mally shrugged. "Small guy, like his name. Small-time."

"Is he mob?"

"Who knows?"

"*You* know. Talk."

"Hell, I suppose he is. So what?"

"I'll tell you so what." Angrily, he threw a handful of sand on the ashes of the fire. "A: The mob makes book you'll never appear at his trial. B: Somebody in the Phoenix P.D. doesn't want you there, either. A plus B equals a tie-in between the mob and the cops. He must be the tie-in, and you must be the one who can prove it."

She gave a yawn, and scoffed. "You sat on your ass all night figuring that out? Congratulations."

"Tell me about DeLucca." His tone did not change, was still steady and quiet.

"What do you want from me?" She kicked a toe into the sand. "I only met the guy once. Jesus, Shockley, I'm no good without a cup of coffee. Will you lay off me?"

"The one time that you met him—what happened? What were the circumstances?"

She sat down a few feet away from him and fondled a stone embedded in the sand. "I don't want to talk about it."

He sprang to his feet. "Don't want to *talk* about it! You don't want to *talk* about it! Look, for all I know, half the goddam police force is crooked, and our lives are on the line because of it, and you just don't want to talk about it!"

"You heard what I said," she said softly. "So forget it."

"Jesus Christ..." he paced away from her, his head tilted back, muttering. Then he came back to her. "Who are you protecting?"

"Nobody."

"Bullshit!"

"Me! I'm protecting me. Okay? Now lay off!"

"Protecting *you?* This is the way you protect *yourself?* Get us both running from a mobile firing squad? Protecting yourself from what? From me? Have *I* tried to run you off the road? Have *I* tried to jump your bones? Have *I* tried to pump you full of holes? Jesus, when are you gonna realize I'm not the enemy!"

"You're not the enemy."

"Jesus, I'll say I'm not. I'm the one who's been protecting you."

"Hooray for Mr. Clean."

"Listen to me, will you?" He squatted down next to her.

"I've got to know what's going on here. Now, what did DeLucca do?"

“I can’t.” She looked at the sand, her fingers working around the stone, finally prying it loose. She rolled it around in her hand. “I can’t tell you.”

Ben studied her. He’d spent a lot of years listening to people talk, judging their emotions for authenticity. He thought her emotions were real.

“You’re the key,” he said, his voice softening. “You’re the only proof, and both sides know it. And our only hope may be for me to know it, too. I’ve got to know what and who we’re dealing with.”

She tossed the small stone up and down, her eyes following it.

“Please,” he said.

The unexpected use of that word made her turn to look at him.

A heavy silence descended. But Shockley knew he was on the edge of something now. His instincts and experience told him not to speak. It was a question of timing. If he kept quiet now, there would be more pressure on her than any words could match.

Mally finally took a deep breath and spoke, her voice quiet, distant. “DeLucca set me up with somebody—you know, a date. Asked me to be ‘special nice’ to him.”

Ben let another few seconds pass. “Who was it?”

“I was never given his name. I wasn’t supposed to know.”

“Someone on the force?” His question came quickly.

“Yes.”

“Vegas?”

She shook her head. “No. Yours. I think it was yours.”

Her “I think” had the force of gospel; she was being absolutely honest now. And as much as he didn’t want to hear it, he knew that was what the answer had to be. The night spent in pensive analysis had left him with that unavoidable conclusion: it had to be his own department. As hard as it was to accept that, the rest would be harder. "What was his name?"

"I told you, I don't know. I wasn't supposed to ask."

He squeezed a thumb and forefinger across his eyes. He *had* already asked her that. It broke the rhythm of his questioning for him to lose concentration that way. He was very tired. "Okay. So what happened?"

She rubbed her thumb absentmindedly across the rough surface of the stone, and her thoughts went back to the vivid, frightful ceremony.

"I went to a hotel room in Vegas. There was... this guy. What can I say? He seemed like... like a decent enough guy. Quiet. I... asked him how he... wanted it. He told me to undress."

Her eyes were glazed with the remembrance of that night.

In deference to her privacy, in recognition of his invasion of it, Ben turned away and looked across the sand.

"Then he had me lie down on the bed... on my stomach.

He got on the bed. I couldn't see him. And he told me to... open my legs."

She stopped, mentally probing what lay ahead, wondering if she had the courage to rid herself of it once and for all. "He took his gun, and he pushed it in... deep... and he held it there with one hand while he... I mean, I could hear what he was doing with his other hand, and he said..."

She stopped again, looking over at Ben, grimacing as if in pain. "He said if I screamed he'd pull the trigger. But," She closed her eyes. "I had to be nice to him because... because Little Angel said... to be nice." Then she concluded quickly. "So when it was over, I dressed and left. That's all."

The stone fell from her hand, and her body sagged with relief.

Ben didn't relax. Her story had moved him to pity for her, but also to anger and disgust. But it was not the point. She had not yet reached the point. That scene was not why they were in danger. It was not because of *what* the john was, but *who.* And beyond the name, it was because of what he could deliver to the mob.

"Little Angel told you to be nice."

She nodded.

"I think he gave you a reason."

She looked at him, her eyes pleading.

"Tell me."

"Because the man could give them the whole city of Phoenix."

He knew why there were tears in her eyes. Her code was that you never tell, not something like that, not in her business. Not for moral reasons, but for simple practical ones. To tell was to call down a death sentence on herself.

But the sentence had already been handed down. And Ben was the only person who might possibly be able to deliver her from it. So she had told.

"Describe him," Ben said firmly.

"Yes." This was easier for Mally. "Fifty, early fifties. Dark brown eyes, black hair with no gray. A face like a stone and a voice..." She paused and shuddered slightly, remembering the voice and searching for the right words to describe it. "It seemed to come from the bottom of a tomb."

Ben closed his eyes in stunned acceptance.

When he opened them, he spoke a single word that brought everything into sharp, brutal focus.

"Blakelock!"

CHAPTER 16

The stark, almost palpable truth lay between the two of them, as if itself a stone in the sand.

To Mally, the name meant nothing. But she could see in Ben's eyes that to him it meant everything. The name echoed in her mind; the vision of Ben's rage and contempt upon uttering it stayed with her. "Who is he?"

"Head of Internal Affairs. The guy who sent me to bring you back."

There was silence between them. For several minutes, as the sun climbed into the early morning sky, they sat staring across the desert hills.

Suddenly the stillness was rent by the roar of an engine being cranked alive.

Shockley immediately had his gun out, moving in front of Mally to protect her.

Soon the first engine was joined by another, and then a third, then several more. The noise came from the other side of a craggy dune a couple of hundred yards away.

"Hogs," Ben said, half to himself.

"What?"

"Hogs, motorcycles. Lots of them. Stay here." He held up his hand. "Stay."

He made a low, dodging run across the arid terrain toward the rocky embankment that separated him from the thunder of the motorcycles. Stumbling occasionally, he reached the top of the incline and peered cautiously over a man-sized rock, letting out a long, slow breath as he took in the scene below him.

Occupying an open acre of desert surrounded by towering pockmarked monoliths of rock was an encampment of bikers, dozens of them.

There were tents, gear, tools, women, and children—all assembled around a scattered core of some fifty highly customized bikes. The bearded, dirty, Viking-like men were either sitting listlessly on the ground with their mommas or straddling their hogs, arms outstretched to the handlebars, hands twitching on the throttles, scraggly heads nodding to the ululating cadence of the machines.

It was an awesome array of men, noise, and color. As Shockley lay assessing the herd of nomads, he heard the sound of slipping gravel behind him. A moment later Mally slid to the ground beside him.

"My God," she whispered as she peered around the rock.

"Stay down."

"I'm sure as hell not going to go down there and wish them all a good morning."

Ben started to stand up. She grabbed his arm and tried to tug him back down, but he shook her off. "Now stay here, dammit!" he barked. "If you show your head, I've got no chance of pulling this off."

"What?" she whispered urgently, "Pulling off what?"

But he was already on his feet and stepping from behind the protection of the boulder.

Squaring his shoulders, he strode briskly down into the tiny valley.

"All right, you mother-jumpers!" His bellowing voice reverberated among the rocks. *"This is a bust!"*

Dozens of heads swung around toward him. Gun in hand, his tall, lean frame silhouetted against the morning sky, he descended into their midst.

"This is a bust!" he repeated.

The bikers and their mommas froze in a still-life tableau.

Advancing steadily toward the stunned group, Ben roared out commands with the authoritative presence of General Patton and the volume of a bullhorn.

"Everybody! Over there! Against the bikes! Hands up, feet spread, and your balls in your pockets! MOVE!"

Mally watched in bug-eyed horror from behind the rock, shaking all over, waiting for the inevitable reaction from the violent bikers that would swallow up Shockley and leave him a bloody blot on the sand.

But as Ben moved on, barking commands, the audacity of his attack forced the startled gathering into a grudging compliance. One by one the bike engines sputtered and died.

The key, Ben knew, was speed—moving so fast and confidently that you gave none of them time to think. Walking among them, gesturing boldly with his Magnum, he kept the hulking men off guard by making them react to his orders.

"Didn't you hear me, Shorty? Move your big butt over there and get those feet spread out! You! Get in gear! Up against that chopper where I can see your hands! You! Get your sleepy ass up off the ground and get over there! You! Quit playin' with yourself! Get your hands out of your pockets and *move!* He turned from one to the other, issuing directives. One biker, a big, pot-bellied man with one eye nearly closed from scars, started to get up as ordered. But as Ben turned away, he grabbed a tire iron and sprang. Ben saw the shadow behind him and spun, ducking away as the tire iron whistled down past his head. Instantly, he brought his leg up in a stiff kick that caught his attacker squarely in the balls, doubling him over and collapsing him backwards—and at the same time emptying the lungs of every male in sight.

Shockley quickly regained his balance, clicked back the hammer of his Magnum, and slowly panned it around at all the staring bikers. His gun was, as always, the crucial advantage of power; and, as always, its power was greatest when it could be held as a threat, and not fired.

"First turkey tries something like that again, I'll shoot him in the balls and shove an apple up his ass." He panned the gun again, locking his eyes on those of each biker in turn.

"Any takers?" He jabbed at each with his gun. "You? You?"

Then he was moving again, always moving, careful not to stand still, never to be a stationary target. He was careful not to stumble, not to miss a beat, to make sure he garbled no words, to keep cool and show complete confidence. But above all, to keep moving. With a consummate combination of skill and daring, he corralled the remaining bystanders up against their bikes.

"You can't do this without a warrant," growled one of the stragglers.

Ben turned slowly toward him and fashioned a smile that spread into a broad sneer. "Man says I can't do this without a warrant." He turned his sneer upon the other bikers, then back to the straggler. "Man don't know jack-shit! Anybody here but me know what the law says?" He scanned their faces again. "Any lawyers here? Who's gonna tell me why I *don't* need a warrant? Who's your lawyer here? Ain't you grimy assholes represented by *counsel?* One of you hunks of buffalo shit gonna tell me? Come on, there's a *reason* why I don't need a warrant. Who's got any brain cells left?"

He paraded up and down in front of the cowed ranks, peering into each face like a drill sergeant. "Give you a clue. The key word is 'reasonable.' That tell you anything? Huh?"

It was all timing, Ben knew—drawing it out just right, knowing when to change tack, knowing when to move, when to stop, when to turn. It was like a dramatic display to hold their attention, keep them guessing. It was a skill few had, a skill of his that had never before been so severely tested.

He stalked up and down in front of them. Then, abruptly, he stopped before one of the larger bikers, a man whose casual bearing and hooded, menacing eyes suggested leadership. It was a good guess that he was the main man.

"You! with the dirty mop for a head! You look almost smart enough. I want to hear it!"

The man, in his mid-twenties, a hint of civilization behind his eyes, stared wordlessly back at Shockley, chewing lazily on something.

Ben knew he had guessed right. "Let's have it, big man!"

He waggled his gun. "I want to hear what entitles me to come in here and bust you any goddam time I like. *Loud!* The answer is, I have a *reasonable what?"*

The man blinked his eyes slowly. "You're nuts, man," he said evenly. "Get off my case."

"The answer is"—Ben moved his Magnum a hand's length forward—"a reasonable what?"

The man shrugged. "Reasonable suspicion," he mumbled, glancing to either side at his cohorts.

"LOUD!"

"Reasonable suspicion," the man spat. "Bull says he's got reasonable suspicion."

"Right!" Shockley stepped back, smiling broadly, mockingly, up and down the line. "Reasonable suspicion! If I have reasonable suspicion a felony's been committed, I can go anywhere at any time and do any goddam thing I want, because I carry this badge and this gun, and because the love of Jesus Christ is in my pretty brown eyes."

He paused, raising his eyebrows, moving his gaze from one man to the next, letting the weight of his statement sink in.

"Now." He rubbed his chin thoughtfully and turned away from them for a moment. His instinct told him that now was the right time to show just how casual he could be, how firmly he had control. He looked back at the bikers. "Now, I'm kinda stuck in a fix here, gentlemen. One of you sad-ass turkeys has committed a felony. That's right. I don't know who, and I don't know when, and I don't even know what the exact felony is—and frankly, I don't give a shit. But one of you's got the mark of Cain on his ass. And that turkey knows who I'm talking about. Doesn't he?"

The only sound was the impatient whine of an infant crying for its mother's tit.

"So it looks like I've gotta bust you *all,* understand?"

He raised his eyebrows. Several bikers scuffed their heavy boots idly in the sand. "However," Ben continued, "you've got a choice. If all of you clear-ass out of here in thirty seconds, I'll let you off with just a warning. If you don't-if you give me any shit at all—a couple of you are gonna find bullets in your legs, and within half an hour there's gonna be more cops and more guns and more dope sniffing dogs and more handcuffs than any of you ever saw in your wildest hallucinations. Do you hear me?"

His gaze turned icy. Several bikers glanced nervously at each other.

"You got thirty seconds!" He spun to face the biker at the end of the row. "Count it off!"

"Sheeeiiit," mumbled the bearded giant, as he spit off to the side.

"Count, cocksucker!"

Ben straightened his gun arm toward the man and sighted down the barrel. From the corner of his eye, he saw the leader nod. The man at the end of the line began to count, evenly, "One... two"—the numbers clicked off with the precision of a metronome—"three... four..."

The camp became a flurry of activity. Bikers pulled on their identifying "color," hastily tied their headbands. With their mommas, they scampered around gathering cooking utensils and clothing and gear, stuffing everything into sacks and saddlebags. Sleeping bags were rolled and lashed into place.

Through it all, Ben kept moving, nudging men from the rear, kicking their boots, prodding them, pointing out forgotten possessions, overseeing the harried exodus with the haughty presence of a pharaoh.

The bikes were starting to pull out when he collared a rider about to start up his engine.

"This bike stays here," Ben said. "You double up with your buddy."

"This is *my* Harley special, Charley."

Ben's Magnum found the soft spot in the biker's armpit. "And this is *my* thirty-eight special, numb-nuts. Off!"

The biker swung off his machine, cursing softly as he climbed aboard another bike behind a buddy. The pair roared off.

Dust swirled around Shockley as dozens of engines ground out an overture of rpm's, the owners jockeying their big machines in graceful arabesques, then heading toward the eastern exit of the valley. The whole band churned out across the desert in a diminishing roll of thunder and disappeared into the hills.

Shockley stood alone beside the commandeered Harley, staring after the vanished bikers. He tucked his gun away.

Then he held his hands out parallel to the ground, a wry smile crossing his face as his hands did just what he had expected.

They trembled.

CHAPTER 17

"Ridiculous! Outrageous! Unbelievably dumb! Shockley, you're totally *insane?* Mally's epithets bounced off the rock walls as she crossed the valley floor.

She stood before him, hands on hips, eyes flashing admiration and fury for what he'd done. "You stupid, witless, brainless, lucky—"

"Thanks for the compliments," he said. "Now get on the bike."

"What?"

"Get on." He swung a leg over the saddle and offered a hand to help her aboard. "Let's go."

"On that?"

"Unless you wanna wait for a boat."

She took his hand. As she stood there, looking at the tired, determined figure who straddled the dirty motorcycle, she felt suddenly as if she'd spent her entire life with him.

"Shockley, you're one hell of a cop."

"Yeah, me and Dirty Harry. Now climb on."

She settled in behind him, her hands sliding to his waist.

"You know how to drive one of these things?"

"We're about to find out, right?" He kicked down the starter and the Harley's engine came to life.

The vibration jounced their bodies as he pulled the big bike forward off its stand. He shifted gears, throttling a little too hard and sending the machine into an accidental spinning Brodie that brought a yelp of surprise from Mally.

Then they were on their way, a tail of dust curling behind them as they left the valley in the direction opposite to the bikers' departure route.

By the time they'd reached the highway, Ben found himself relaxing astride the noisy chopper.

It reminded him of when he was a kid, when he had occasionally "borrowed" a motor scooter or motorcycle, loving the freedom and independence he felt as he roared or putted, depending on the vehicle, out of town and onto country roads. Once he and another kid had managed to find two bikes together; they had gone racing off, leaning around corners and dragging their inside feet to keep balance, bouncing their front wheels into the air whenever a bump in the road gave them sufficient lift, dazzling themselves with their daring and expertise.

Now, remembering those feelings of freedom and independence, Ben wished he could feel them again.

But his freedom now was only that of a hunted animal; his independence was erased by the presence of Mally, by all the burdens and obligations she imposed.

Still, they were moving, which raised his spirits.

Squinting against the wind, the sleeves of his coat billowed by the constant rush of air, Ben guided them along the asphalt strip. On either side stretched the desert, its landscape a study in deception, a sinister fraud of lifelessness. For though the sands that flanked them gave the illusion of being empty and barren, they were in fact teeming with life—cunning predators constantly on the lookout for prey or enemy.

The similarity to his own position was startlingly clear to Shockley. Until some forty-eight hours ago, he had believed that he knew the dimensions of his life very well—almost too well, so well he felt confined by them. He had thought he led a straight-line existence that had long ago run out of surprises. But then came Josie's promotion, and his own assignment to deliver one "Gus" Mally to a court of law. And like the desert, his life had become alive with stalking danger.

There was, however, a single prominent exception that struck him: in the desert, animals knew which species were friends and which were potential enemies. They were born with that knowledge in their blood and bones and tissues.

But he wasn't allowed that luxury. His own kind had turned against him.

And ironically, his own kind could be hunting him right now, somewhere out in that same desert. Any human beings he ran into right now he would have to assume were enemy.

Yet somehow he still felt there was one he could trust.

One among the pack of Judas goats who wouldn't lead him to the slaughter.

It was his only chance—*their* only chance—and as he felt Mally's grip tighten around his waist, felt her head lean against his back, he hoped to hell that what he was about to do wouldn't get them both killed.

Mally enjoyed the warmth of his body, and she held her self tight against him. For so long the touch of a male had been an unpleasant part of her business, which was the delivery of pleasure at the cost of it to herself. She had begun to fear, as she found common among her friends in the business, that she might never truly enjoy a man again.

But this way, feeling his warmth through his clothes, hugging him from the back, it was just impersonal enough to allow her to enjoy it. And she felt that she was a woman still —would be, for the right man.

Not that Shockley was the right man, of course. But he

was the first man she'd been with in a long time who wasn't paying her for the rental of her body.

In fact, he wasn't paying her for anything. And she was the most serious kind of trouble to him.

It crossed her mind from time to time as they rode that if she could escape from him, at least she would stop being a problem for him. Maybe she owed him that.

But there were two things about Ben Shockley: one, she didn't think she *could* escape from him, not with his talent for hanging onto her; two, she no longer *wanted* to get away from him, because she had become convinced that he wanted to survive just as much as she did, that she had a better chance with him.

Simple as that.

The helicopter was a four-place Sikorsky, bearing no markings.

It hovered above the burnt-out campfire, circling the remains as if it were a buzzard over carrion flesh. The pilot skillfully maneuvered the craft at low altitude, playing the foot pedals and hand levers deftly. His lone passenger steadied a Winchester 30-30 across his lap as he peered through silvered sunglasses at the ground below.

It wasn't long before the man in the sunglasses found what he was looking for: two distinct sets of footprints leading away from the campfire and up a sandy incline a couple of hundred yards away.

Following the tracks, the 'copter skimmed across the crest of the hill and swooped down into the tiny valley, covering the territory in ever-narrowing concentric circles.

At first glance, the markings the man saw looked like a meaningless conglomeration of criss-crossing lines, but closer evaluation revealed that they all converged on a similar point of exit at the eastern mouth of the valley.

The pilot banked for a second pass, and the passenger pointed suddenly to his left, indicating that he wanted a look at some fresh piece of evidence that had caught his eye.

Suspended above the earth in their lucite bubble, the two men scoured the terrain, satisfied that they'd found what they needed.

Then, with a chatter of its rotors as they adjusted to forward flight, the Sikorsky followed the new trail: a single track leading to the west exit of the valley.

It was a small, ramshackle town. Ben drove up the single street and stopped in front of a small, gray, beat-up general store. There was a phone booth outside.

He parked the bike at the curb and headed for the booth.

"Get us something to eat," he told Mally. "Hamburgers, anything."

Nodding, she trotted up the steps and disappeared into the store.

Ben's coins clanked into the pay phone. Waiting, he gazed through the glass of the booth at their motorcycle, beyond it the scruffy foothills that backdropped the sleepy, ragtag town that they had stumbled upon.

His connection was made. "Give me Detective Josephson," he said, "Metro Squad."

There was a pause, and then Josie's familiar voice crackled across the line. "Detective Josephson speaking."

For an instant, Ben almost hung up, doubting whether he dared identify himself to anyone. Doubting whether he had the right to involve Josie in this. Doubting... But he had no choice. "Josie, it's me."

"Ben?" The word leaped across the distance. "Jeeesus, Ben..." Josie lowered his voice to a near-whisper. "There's an APB out on you! Where the hell are you? Why the hell did you do it?"

"Do what?"

"That sheriff's deputy, last night—why in God's name did you have to kill him?"

"I didn't kill anybody, Josie."

"But they, everybody said... Jesus Christ, Ben, they found the damn *body. Somebody* killed the poor bastard."

"It wasn't me, Josie."

"But then, who did it?"

"It's Blakelock."

"Who?"

"Blakelock. Internal Affairs."

"Christ almighty, Ben! He's a lieutenant commander!"

"I don't give a shit what he is. He's tied in with the mob. He's trying to nail me, Josie. Me and the girl."

Josie's voice whined with bewilderment. "Girl? What girl? What do you mean, nail you? What the hell's going on? What the hell are you talking about?"

Ben rapped his fist against the side of the phone, jangling it. So much had happened. "Okay, Josie, I'll take it from the beginning. Don't say anything. Just listen..."

The pencil-like track across the desert floor came to an abrupt halt at the highway, forcing the stalking helicopter to dip and circle back over the area.

"Which way?" the pilot asked above the clatter of the rotors.

The passenger remained silent, mentally computing the backroads and tributaries that fed off the highway in each direction, and the various likelihoods and tendencies and options pertaining to his prey. Then he jerked his thumb to the left.

The pilot nodded and pivoted the Sikorsky. A glint of sunlight filtered through the bubble and bounced off the identical pairs of silvered sunglasses worn by the two men.

They flew at moderate speed for a minute or so. Then the passenger held up his hand. The pilot pulled the plane into a hover.

The passenger narrowed his eyes in thought. He rubbed a hand over his mouth, keeping the other hand fondly on the rifle in his lap.

Then he hooked a thumb over his shoulder, toward the rear.

The pilot pivoted the plane 180 degrees, and they moved off in the other direction.

The passenger bared his teeth in a confident smile. He nodded, pointed ahead, and formed his thumb and forefinger into a letter O.

The pilot nodded and smiled also, and gave his passenger a thumbs-up.

Ben cradled the phone on his shoulder as he nervously rubbed his hands together. "...so Blakelock knows that if she testifies, she'll torpedo him. That's why he's trying to ice her. And now he knows that *I'll* torpedo him, anyway. That's why he's trying to ice me. Either one of us can destroy him."

He had rushed through the explanation, realizing as he did that he'd be hard-pressed to believe it himself if he were on the other end of the line.

"Ben, you haven't been..."

"No, Josie, sober as a judge, all the way." He wasn't even annoyed by Josie's suggestion. This was an awful lot to handle, and Josie had a right to dig at it, probe it, question it.

"Holy Jesus." Josie's voice was filled with quiet awe. "You got any idea what this means?"

"Damn right I do. It means me and the witness are as good as dead. Unless you help me. Do you hear what I'm telling you?"

"I hear you, Ben."

A faraway, rhythmic sound crept into the confines of the phone booth.

"And do you believe me?"

"Yeah, I believe you." Josie spoke the words slowly, evenly, precisely, each one a nail in the bargain he was making. "Of course I do."

"Okay."

"But Jesus, Ben, what the hell are you gonna... I mean, what can I do? Believe me, I am willing to do anything required, anything you want, to help you. But who the hell can I take something like this to?"

Ben's mind was already running down the list of possibilities—he had started even before making the call—but virtually every name that occurred to him was a potential risk. He had no idea how deep the thing went, how far it had spread, how many were already in the net. At least Josie wasn't in it, he was sure of that. But who? "I don't know, Josie..." he began.

The sound that had begun as a distant intrusion was much closer now, louder, forcing him to cover his free ear.

"Ben? You still there?"

He glanced up and saw the approaching helicopter. "I can barely hear you! But get to someone! I don't know who—just do it!"

The plea came across to Josie as garbled fragments of sentences. Then there was an unidentifiable noise in the background, followed by a single distinct, crack.

Ben dropped the receiver.

The bullet had spiked through two sides of the booth, missing his neck by inches.

CHAPTER 18

"Ben?" Josie's voice cried into the empty booth from the dangling telephone receiver.

Shockley lunged through the door and hit the ground as three more rounds crashed into the aluminium-and-glass enclosure. Then he was up, scrambling across the flimsy porch of the old general store.

As he burst in, Mally was just turning away from the small lunch counter with an armload of food. Ben grabbed her wrist, sending their lunch flying, and pulled her on a dead run out the door and down the steps.

The Sikorsky was just a few feet off the ground, and about to touch down on the dusty main street, when Shockley and Mally dashed out of the general store. The men in the helicopter were caught off guard, having prepared themselves to land and carry out their mission inside the store. The craft yawed violently, one landing skid touching the ground at an oblique angle and sending another of the passenger's shots astray.

The pilot didn't know whether to land or hover. He beat on the passenger's shoulder to get his attention for directions, and the passenger missed another shot.

Ben and Mally raced for the parked motorcycle. They vaulted aboard, and he jammed his heel down on the starter.

He spun the bike around and took off, the rear wheel spewing dirt and sand and launching the front wheel off the ground for the first few yards of his acceleration.

Mally clutched frantically at his suit coat as they sped away, burying her face in his back, barely able to comprehend the swift chain of events that had her calmly buying their lunch one moment, then fleeing for her life the next.

The hog roared down the quiet street, its engine thundering furiously in their ears. Ben made no attempt to avoid the few amazed spectators caught in the action; he hoped their reflexes would save them. Bystanders dived right and left for cover.

Even over the din of the bike, Mally could feel the ominous presence of the tracking 'copter behind them, the thump of its rotors like the footfalls of a pursuing beast. Her whole body was rigid with terror; her nerves sang with fear, her mind reeled with hopeless dismay. With each succeeding second she waited for the searing pain of an exploding shell, knowing it was coming, wishing at least that it would all end swiftly, without lingering agony.

The narrow road was filled suddenly with an oncoming pickup truck. The rattling vehicle chugged down the middle of the street, its elderly driver gaping beneath two bushy white eyebrows at the fantastic sight of the speeding motorcycle and the following helicopter.

Ben stared at the driver's face, leaning in disbelief toward the windshield.

"Move, damn you!" Ben's words were swallowed up by the relentless cacophony of pistons and rotor blades and wind.

Swiftly judging the clearance on either side of the pick up, Ben swerved his bike to the left just as a shot from the helicopter skipped off the asphalt and shattered the right headlight of the truck. For an agonizing moment, it seemed the truck would lurch directly into their path, but then the old man pulled the wheel sharply in the opposite direction, jumping the curb on the other side of the street and sending a smashed mailbox bouncing down the sidewalk.

Mally dug her fingers deep into Ben's waist as they careened off the main street onto a dirt crossing. The pitch of the Sikorsky's engine altered as it pulled around to follow their flight.

Ben twisted the throttle wide open, wondering whether the venerable Harley could stand the high rpm's.

The stock of the Winchester braced firmly against his shoulder, the sniper tried to sight the dodging target below, his eyes steady behind the silvered sunglasses. It was a challenge to him—no more, no less. It was simply his skill and the pilot's against that of the nameless man on the motorcycle. That lives were at stake was no consequence; he'd been paid to deliver a service, and though the quarry was putting up a good fight, the odds were heavily in the hunter's favor.

In fact, he knew he would not fail. In this business, men who failed on such a mission no longer existed; the fact that he was still in the business and on this assignment was evidence that he had never failed. No prey had ever escaped him, whether his means was gun, knife, or bomb. The method was always up to him. This time he had chosen the pilot, a man of great skill and no memory, which made him valuable and safe; and he had chosen the rifle—his best weapon.

It was simply a matter of time now until one of the bullets struck home. That was a foregone conclusion in the sniper's precise, unfeeling brain.

. . .

The beat of the cycle pounded through Ben and Mally as he veered the Harley right and left, bullets excavating chunks of earth in the wake of the bike's erratic path. The wind bit into his face and peeled his lips back into a grimace.

The surrounding foothills were their only chance of escape, but even that shelter was still a good two hundred yards away—more than enough space in which to die. But there were no options. Ben imagined the gunman reloading, hated how casually the bastard could sight down the barrel and squeeze the trigger. No matter how difficult a darting target they were, the gunman would bracket their moves and eventually home in.

Still, he would make it tough for the bastards. He would make them sweat. They would have to work their asses off to get him.

Easing the throttle back a fraction, he pivoted the bike into an abrupt, sliding, arm-wrenching 180-degree turn, his left leg cocked to slide his heel along the ground for balance.

The combination of the spinning bike's centrifugal force and Mally's awkward wrestling to stay aboard nearly flung them both from their seats.

His leg barely held under the strain of the turn, but he found the strength to right the bike and push off, and they were again one with the roaring cycle.

The maneuver gained them a precious few seconds on the 'copter as it banked, skimmed wide on the air, and changed course.

Abandoning the road, Ben barreled the Harley toward the nearest outcropping of hills. Twisted forms of cacti seemed to point the way like ranks of crippled sentinels.

Bouncing across the rugged terrain, the gritty taste of sand and bile in her mouth, Mally could do nothing to help their escape. She could only hold on and wait; everything was up to Ben. She couldn't stop herself from picking out patches of sand in front of her—one marked by a low, anvil-like rock, another highlighted by sparkling fragments of mica—and imagining that each would be the spot where she would die.

But somehow each death-plot whistled past without claiming her. And so there was a tiny spark of hope.

She held on tight and felt the warmth of Ben's body.

Come on, Shockley. Unspoken words, but she knew he heard them above the clamor of engines, knew he sensed her encouragement, however slight. *Come on, you ragged-assed, pinch-brained cop! Get us the hell out of here!* She dug her fingers into his waist, communicating her will to live.

The Sikorsky stalked them from fifty yards behind and a hundred feet above the sand, gaining steadily.

The Winchester spat round after round at the scurrying beetle below. Neither hunter spoke, but the pilot was well aware of his passenger's growing frustration as each shot missed the quicksilver target. He was used to a clean, efficiently executed job, the gunman was, not a cat-and-mouse game that forced him to do his work from a yawing, pitching machine that dangled him above the earth—at least not for this long a time. Prior experiences with this method had been much simpler: find the prey, drop down suddenly like a hawk, squeeze off the handful of shots necessary for demolition, then rise and fly away, go home, report, and draw the final installment of pay.

Thirty yards, and still the gunman was denied a hit. Why couldn't the pilot keep the goddam thing any steadier? The gunman began to jerk the trigger back like a petulant customer at a firing range, swearing angrily with each faulty shot.

The pilot sweated, licked his lips, and narrowed his eyes in even deeper concentration.

Suddenly, the gunman found the motorcycle square in his sights. For a fraction of a second, he saw the woman's spine as if it were frozen by the lens of a stop-motion camera. His finger pulled smoothly back against the trigger. His mind had already recorded the gory result.

"Goddammit!' The blast of the rifle came just as the helicopter made a stomach-flipping, radical tilt turning the gunman's world upside down. The pilot had just barely avoided the twin peaks that bordered the narrow ravine into which the motorcycle plunged for cover.

Now the aircraft veered back down into the ravine. The gunman again thrust the barrel of his rifle out the port and fired in an uncontrolled frenzy.

Below, Shockley played the bike across the turning, twist ing canyon floor.

Bullets flattened themselves against the rocky slopes, whistling, whining, and ricocheting in an unearthly symphony that Mally thought would drive her mad. But above it all, she heard the single, distinct, metallic "thunk" of one bullet as it rocketed into the Harley's engine.

Ben felt the pulse of their powerplant lose its rhythm.

Their speed slackened. The bike coughed and sputtered like a wheezing old man. But it didn't stop. The engine regained some of its momentum. Ben played the throttle and gears skillfully in a desperate effort to get them around the final curve in the snaking canyon.

Moving in for the death blow, the Sikorsky swooped even lower, the rifleman already feeling the first trace of the heady sensation that always accompanied a kill. It was an orgasm of power, and he sighted once again along the barrel of his Winchester, he relished the taste of what was to come.

Ben slid the bike into the final curve, without thinking

about what might be waiting for them beyond, when they were again out in the open.

Suddenly the protective canyon walls fell away, disappeared like a prop in a magician's act.

But what Ben saw sail by above his head flashed like a miracle.

The helicopter swept around the curve behind them, the two pairs of eyes behind silvered sunglasses squinting, the two mouths smiling in anticipation of the kill.

But then the eyes of both hunters bulged. Directly in front of the plane's nose, the heavy gray cables of a high-tension line sagged across the mouth of the canyon.

CHAPTER 19

Ben felt a sweet stab of satisfaction and relief when he heard the collision.

The nerve-jangling crackle of unleashed high-voltage electricity swiveled Mally's head around, and she watched in fascinated horror as the helicopter became the nucleus of a searing, blue-white explosion, then plummeted to earth in a deluge of dismembered rotors and tubular steel.

The desert accepted the burnt offering in stoic silence.

Mally buried her face tearfully in Ben's back as they rode away from the awful scene.

The desert seemed flat and arid as the skin of hell, and endless before them.

They'd been riding for half an hour since the helicopter died, half an hour of luxurious uninterrupted freedom that even the desolate terrain couldn't mar. Slowly, the sense of impending death had slipped from Mally, though she knew that their marathon was far from over, that it would still quite probably end with their destruction. Yet she worshipped this interval of peace, no matter how brief and fragile it might be.

Shockley, however, was occupied with concern about how much longer he could nurse their wounded Harley along before it gave them up to the desert. Already the vibrations of the bike were communicating missed beats and subtle lags of power. The fuel gauge still registered half full, but that meant little if the engine was dying. And Ben was certain that it was in its death throes.

He searched the horizon for any irregularity that might signal civilization. As he had for the last five minutes, he concentrated on an elongated, almost lifeless shape in the far distance.

It had entered his view as an umber filament, a slender, earth-toned thread carelessly flung across the landscape. At first he had taken little notice of it, but as he became more and more aware of the bike's waning power, he had focused on whatever it was as a possible means of salvation; he had concentrated on it, aimed for it, almost without conscious realization of what he was doing. He'd said nothing to Mally because it might *be* nothing. It could be a mirage, a geologic fault, a meaningless discoloration in the sand, a reflection from some distortion in the sky.

Still, he headed for it, trying to resist the distressing thought that he really didn't have a plan. He had been reacting defensively to one attack after another, and had so far been successful. But he couldn't remain on the defensive forever, without finally losing. Somehow he had to gain the offensive.

But for that he needed a plan—step one, step two. It was no longer the relatively simple matter of eluding various traps and finally delivering Mally as promised and ordered.

The job was more massive, intricate, ominous. He needed time to sit down and work it out, plot his goal and his moves toward it.

And yet, all they were doing was riding a fatally crippled

motorcycle across an unknown stretch of desert toward—what?

Were they escaping, or merely sliding deeper into oblivion? Was this ribbon on the horizon a solution to their problems?

Or was it a solution to the problems of their enemy?

Or was it nothing at all?

Then, gradually, the faint umber slash of color began to resolve itself into contour and shape—and it was moving. Now Ben could see it: a long caravan of freight cars trundling their way south.

Mally too had become aware of the Harley's sputtering and missing. "How much longer have we got?" she yelled.

"Not a hell of a lot, that's for sure."

"You're one of the all-time great optimists, you know that, Shockley?"

"What?"

"Never mind. Where're we going?"

He didn't answer. He opened the throttle wide, and the Harley picked up speed, coughing with the effort.

"Hey!" Mally called. "Give the thing half a chance, will you?"

"Shut up and hold on—we got a train to catch!"

Mally saw the rambling freight for the first time and dipped her head under Ben's arm to see better. For a few seconds she stared into the wind, blinking away tears to focus on the apparition.

"You're goddam crazy, Shockley! We can't catch that thing! We'll never make it!"

"Nag, nag, nag."

They bounded across the desert, Mally watching the sand blur past beneath her, Ben's attention locked on the long line of cars still a quarter of a mile away.

The train whistle sounded—a quick, short blast followed by a long, full-bodied tone. Perhaps the sound had no purpose but to clear the track of some frightened animal. But to Shockley it was a mournful signal that he would be too late, that his efforts were a waste of time and hope. Yet it was a challenge. And the fact that his own police department was betting against him prodded him forward. He leaned into the wind, gritting his teeth, determined to catch the train.

The closer they got, the more formidable the task appeared. The freight might just as well have been a mountain range they had to scale. The cars towered above them, an impregnable, gliding fortress. There was no hospitality in this lifeless hulk, no welcome for human beings running for their lives.

The clamor of steel wheels rolling against steel rails jangled in their ears, grew in intensity, and finally eclipsed the feeble sputterings of the Harley.

Ben felt the bike's engine die beneath him, the vibrations through the handlebars ceasing with a final shudder. The speed of the cycle quickly slackened, and Mally's grip at the waist became a fearful, questioning clawing.

"Bail out!" He bellowed the order over the noise of the train.

If she thought about it, she wouldn't do it. So instantly, without calculation, Mally threw herself from the coasting bike. She felt Ben tumble off with her. They rolled like tumbleweeds over the sand.

Then Shockley was scrambling to his feet and hauling her up by her arm. She felt a sharp, shooting pain in her shoulder as he yanked her off the ground, and then she was stumbling after him toward the steadily moving train.

Running at a tangent to the freight, they still had some fifty yards to cover, and even at its leisurely pace of twenty miles per hour, most of the cars had already passed them by.

Setting his sights on the partially open door of a clattering cattle car near the end, Ben pumped his legs mercilessly through the loose sand. Mally stumbled behind him, still holding his hand.

This car would be their one chance; if they missed it, the train would be gone. They dug through the soil, gasping for breath. Hot air entered and left their lungs in fatigue-ridden gasps; blood pounded in their ears and eyes; muscles rebelled in pain and exhaustion. And still the train moved inexorably by, heedless and heartless, a great, rusting steel beast taking with it their last chance for escaping the desert.

But Ben kept up the pace. His burning, throbbing eyes told him that the distance was narrowing, and a vivid image of a complacent Blakelock pushed him beyond his own tolerance, drew him ever closer to the open door of the cattle car.

He was almost within reach when his eyes were blinded by the sting of his own sweat. The train was reduced to a shape less mass of dirty brown, enveloped by the relentless hammering of its wheels against the rails, the groaning of the walls of its cars.

He reached out with his free arm. The metal handhold on the side of the car was little more than a foot from his grasp.

Mally faltered. "I... can't!" Her voice was a parched moan. She missed a single step, and that stumble dragged Ben's extended fingers six inches farther from the car.

He dared not let her hand loose from his; to reach the train without her was pointless. He pulled her. He wanted to say something, yell something, to bludgeon her with the understanding that they could make it—that they *had* to make it—but all he could do was run. Run to try to close the precious gap.

He wasn't even sure he was running. He couldn't feel his legs any more, just the clots of pain they transmitted. His head was beginning to fog. His whole body was deserting him. There was no more left in it to give. He began to welcome the final stride, the headlong plunge into the abrasive sand, where he could lie in defeat, and rest, and breathe.

Blakelock had won; the smart money was about to get paid off. Blakelock had beaten him without even really knowing him; he had guessed right about Ben Shockley.

No. His legs were somehow still under him, still moving. He forced himself to focus for one last time on the mocking image of the car, the taunting black hole of the open door.

Then, from within the shadows of the car, there emerged the simple shape of an outstretched hand; its grasp would be victory.

CHAPTER 20

His mouth open in a silent plea, Ben grabbed the offered hand. The strong pull of sinewy arm dragged him forward until he felt the impact of the floor's edge against his stomach. With the assistance of his unseen benefactor, he heaved himself up and into the moving car.

But in the effort he lost Mally's grip. He spun around on his belly and thrust his head and shoulders out of the door.

Mally had somehow caught the metal rung. She held on, her feet dragging in the sand, her eyes closed. Her hands began to slip from the hold. Ben lunged and seized her wrist. Her eyes opened in weary acknowledgment: he had her, but she couldn't help.

Ben had no strength to pull her in.

But then two other pairs of hands reached out, took her arms, and hauled her aboard.

They collapsed in a mosaic of arms and legs, the bruises and scrapes from their entry not yet registering their pain. As Ben rolled over, his handcuffs jarred loose from his belt and clattered across the grimy floor.

Gasping for breath, his muscles trembling uncontrollably, he managed to raise himself on his forearms, his head still hanging toward the floor.

"Thanks, buddy." The sentence was a dry, mumbled croak.

"We seen you comin'. Seen you for a long ways."

There was something about the sound of the man's voice that jogged Ben's memory. Slowly he lifted his head—and looked directly into the yellow-toothed grin of the biker whose hog he'd commandeered back in the desert valley.

The biker's face was a mass of welts and cuts, swirls of purple and black bruises around small cakes of red and black dried blood. He was flanked by two brawny, dull-eyed hoboes, one of them fondling Ben's handcuffs with all the anticipation of a demented child about to pull the wings from a captive insect.

"Looks like we got ourselves a bull," the hobo said, his eyes darting back and forth from the handcuffs to Ben.

"Yessir," the biker said, grinning. "It's like I told these fellers here, we was about to get ourselves a bull, a bull I wanted real bad."

Suddenly, the three ragged figures dove at Ben, crashing into his exhausted body with a fury he couldn't begin to match.

Mally screamed. But a back-handed blow from the biker sent her tumbling across the width of the car. She recovered in time to see one of the hoboes swing the haft of a mucking shovel against the base of Shockley's skull.

The lopsided fight was over as quickly as it had begun, and Mally watched with horror as the three men hauled Ben's semi-conscious form erect and bound his outstretched arms to the slatted wall of the cattle car with baling wire. He hung there as if the victim of a crude crucifixion.

The biker grabbed a handful of Ben's hair and slammed his head against the wooden slats.

"What the hell you doin' chasin' trains when you got my hog to ride, huh, bull? You motherfucker! First you steal my bike, then you wreck it!" He jammed his fist into Shockley's stomach, doubling him over so that the wire bit sharply into his wrists.

"Stop it! Leave him alone!" Mally bounded across the car. "You bastards!"

Again, she felt the leathery backhand of the biker across her face.

"Spunky little girl you got there, pig," the biker said. He reached inside Shockley's coat and slid the Magnum from its pouch.

He examined the gun closely, then weaved the barrel under Ben's nose. "Had yourself a lot of fun this morning, didn't you? Rousted us all real nice and made off with my hog. Sent me off to ride behind my buddy, all neat and nice. 'Cept that we don't have no room for extra riders in my bunch. Did you know that, pig? One chopper, two men. One man don't make it. And the one that don't make it is the one whose chopper it *ain't.*" He leaned close in. "Take a look at my face, pig! That's the face of the man who didn't make it, ain't it? The face of the man who didn't have no bike of his own!"

The biker worked his lips, then spat into Shockley's face.

"And *you're* the reason I don't have no bike of my own. Ain't that so, *pig?*"

He stepped back and waggled the gun. "Well, now"—his smile wiggled like a garter snake—"I got a little news for you. I'm here to tell you there's justice in the world. Yessir. Just like I told the fellers here, when we seen you comin'. Justice. And I can't think of anybody better than me to pass it out."

He nodded slowly, baring his teeth, and tossed the Magnum butt-first to one of the hoboes. "Know what I'm gonna do?" He paused, letting the question dangle in the air. "I'm gonna castrate this here bull. Yessir. Gonna relieve him of his manhood. Gonna cut off his balls and stuff "em in his pocket, so he can play with "em, and remember who put "em there."

A giggle emerged from the hobo holding Ben's handcuffs,

and a fleck of spittle dribbled down his chin. He turned his head slowly away from Ben and looked at Mally. His eyes widened; his lips parted and then came together; his cheeks twitched, and he scratched his groin.

The biker stuck a hand in the back pocket of his dungarees and took out a straight razor that he flipped open with a casual flick of the wrist. He tested the blade with his thumb, still staring at Shockley. Ben tugged futilely at the taut wire that held him. He knew the man wasn't putting on an act; he knew bike gangs, knew the sick cruelty they were capable of. He had been the one to rescue an unfortunate girl—too late, as it turned out—who had happened to walk past a bunch of bikers one night at just the wrong time. Before Ben had received the call and arrived, she had suffered such unbelievable and savage degradation that she had been confined ever since in an institution, unable to recall her own name. And Ben had seen how they could turn their savagery upon themselves in brutal assaults, regardless of limbs and organs and even life itself. What this bastard had suffered at the hands of his own band of brothers was nothing; they had only roughed him up and tossed him out.

Ben knew that this man would easily be capable of what he threatened. For him, it would be a minor operation.

Ben tugged and pushed at the taut wires.

"Gettin' a little nervous, are you?" The biker's voice was sugary. "Well, that's entirely natural. I can understand it. I would be myself, knowing what's gonna happen. See, I ain't a professional at this kind of thing. Never done it myself before. Only *seen* it done. Oh, I picked up a couple of pointers watchin' it before. But what I mean is, I might be just a little messy and slow, it bein' my first time and all."

He stropped the blade against his pants. "My razor might be a little on the dull side. But don't let that worry you, 'cause I plan to do a first-class job. No matter how long it takes."

With his free hand, he reached out and grabbed the handcuffs from the hobo. "Get his pants down."

His mouth wet with tiny bubbles, the grinning hobo shuffled over to Ben and began to work at the buckle of his slacks. The hobo's greasy fingers were gnarled; his long fingernails were like claws.

"Are you guys just a bunch of *faggots?"* Mally's voice rang out above the steady banging of the cattle car along the iron rails.

One by one, the two hobos and the biker turned in her direction.

She stood with her feet spread, her head cocked. Her gaze never left their leering faces as she casually undid the buttons on her blouse. With each deliberate movement of her fingers, the fabric parted a little more, until it hung loosely from her shoulders and revealed the full, round, inner arcs of her bare breasts.

"If you want to play with boys," she said languidly, "go ahead. Be fairies if you want. But personally, I'm into real *men.* I don't ever seem to get enough. I'd actually like to see if you've got anything besides rusty plumbing between your legs."

Brazenly, she shrugged off her blouse.

The hobo's hands went slack at Shockley's belt as he stared open-mouthed at the half-nude woman.

The other hobo let the barrel of the Magnum he was holding droop toward the floor. His mouth worked feverishly. "Let's get her," he grunted.

"I've got work to do!" the biker rasped. He swung the razor over his head. "I got me a *job!"*

Mally unsnapped her jeans and pulled down the zipper.

"How about it, dudes? You got anything to show me, or not?"

Both hoboes danced unevenly in place, breathing hard.

"He'll still be there when we get finished," whined one.

"Yeah, yeah," moaned the other. "Plenty of time, come on. I cain't stand it no more."

They moved a step toward Mally. Realizing that he'd been upstaged, and wanting an attentive audience when he performed his sadistic ritual on Ben, the biker narrowed his eyes as he looked at the two hoboes. Then he turned his head toward Mally.

She waggled her finger at him. "How about you, Mister Bikeman? You got anything to show me, before I change my mind and put all my goodies back in their wrappings? Or is it just your two buddies here who can get it up?"

The biker bared his teeth in a mean smile. He closed the razor and shoved it back in his pocket. He reached out and grabbed the nearer hobo's shoulder and spun him around.

He put his hand over the Magnum the hobo was holding and raised it slowly until it was even with Shockley's chest.

"You keep that on him nice and steady, you hear?"

"What the hell?" the man whined, "I want some *too.*"

"You'll get your turn, don't you worry."

The biker and the other hobo advanced slowly toward Mally. Ben watched them helplessly, slowly turning his wrists in the wires.

They were at her like a pair of starving scavengers, groaning and screeching, grappling at her with arms and legs.

She tried to hide the terror in her eyes as they pulled down her jeans and pawed wildly at her breasts.

The three of them tumbled to the floor, the men's hands clawing at her crotch, ripping off her panties. The noxious breath of the biker filled Mally's nostrils. She gagged as he forced his mouth over hers. She felt her legs being pried apart, felt fingers try to enter her, missing, forcing; then something else, larger, not quite inside…

The hobo holding the gun on Ben watched the panting, snarling tangle of bodies for a few moments. He danced nervously around, saliva dripping from his mouth. He moaned, then glanced at Ben. "Shit, mister, you ain't goin' nowheres."

Dropping the Magnum, he moved tentatively toward the action, then knelt beside Mally and began caressing the inside of her one free leg as a child might stroke a kitten's coat.

She was grateful—God, how ironic!—that there were so many upon her. No one could place himself right; no one could achieve what they all were after—each body interfered with the bodies of the others.

And it was taking precious time, time so precious that she was offering herself to buy it, time for some deliverance she knew was not going to come…

Ben forced his eyes shut, plunged forward, leaned back, plunged forward again, putting sudden, repeated strains on the wires that lashed him to the side of the rumbling car.

The pain came in waves, shooting down his arms and into his torso. The thin wires sliced into his wrists, and he felt the warm trickle of blood mat his shirtsleeves and snake its way down to his elbows.

He didn't know, didn't care, what he was severing, whether arteries or veins; he didn't know whether he would live or die for his efforts. He kept hearing the small animal sounds of horror and suffering that marked Mally's sacrifice.

He was unaware of how many times he lunged against the wires, or how long it took; it seemed an eternity of countless swings. He rocked back and forth, spraying sweat and tears, hoping desperately that the sapping of his blood and strength would not deny him a few more tries, a few more tries…

Then the click of the left wire snapping echoed in his ear like a gunshot.

Frantically, he undid the other wire, stopped for his gun, and sprang for the pile of bodies.

He ripped the top hobo from the mass and rammed the barrel of the Magnum against his temple.

"GET OFF HER!" His shout had the volume of a thunderclap.

The two remaining attackers froze, staring up in disbelief.

"If you bastards move, if you even blink, your partner's brains are gonna cover half the state!"

There was a moment of absolute silence.

Then, like lightning, the biker snapped open his razor and held its blade poised over Mally's jugular. "Fuck yourself, bull. Me and missy here, we're leavin' together!"

"You draw one drop of blood from her and you're all dead meat."

"And so is she, bull, so is she."

The tableau held for several breaths.

Suddenly the biker screamed; Mally had bitten deep into his wrist. She kicked him off and rolled away.

The biker leaped to his feet; he crouched, his razor waving in his hand. Then he sprang.

Ben's Magnum bucked in his hand.

The biker staggered back.

The Magnum exploded again.

The biker tumbled over backwards and disappeared out the open doorway.

Ben waved his gun at the two hoboes huddled in the corner. "Over to the door!"

They bumped into each other as they scampered over.

"Now jump."

"No!" said one, shaking his head.

"I ain't goin" out there!" moaned the other.

"We'll get all busted up!" whined the first.

"Only if you're lucky!" Ben snapped.

"You're a cop, man. That's murder."

"No, murder's what's going to happen to you if you don't go out that door. *Move!*"

Ben raised his foot and jammed it into the first hobo's belly, sending him out. The second man immediately turned and jumped out after him.

For a moment Ben stood staring after them. Then he turned. "Mally..."

She cowered at the far side of the car, not looking at him.

"It's okay," he said softly. "Everything's okay. We made it... again."

She looked up, her face stained with tears. "We made it," she said mechanically. "Yes."

"Okay."

He would have liked to hold her, to crush her to him, to thank her, to apologize, to somehow atone, to erase the awful look of despair in her eyes. But there was nothing he could do, no way to approach her, no point in talk just now.

"Get dressed," he said, and gave her the privacy of his back.

CHAPTER 21

They rode in silence, their backs resting against the wall of the car. Exhaustion and nightmares pulled Mally in and out of a restless sleep. Then, gradually, she began to slough off the remnants of the incident like dead, flaking tissue.

After about an hour the train began to slow, and Ben leaned out the door to see the outlines of a town in the distance.

He shook her shoulder gently to wake her. For a moment, her eyes blazed with the terror of a recall. Then she focused on Ben's face and heaved a little sigh of relief.

"Time to get off," he said.

"Okay. Why?" Her mind was still foggy.

"We're coming to a town."

"Any idea where we are?"

"Nope. But we're not going to ride into the station to find out."

"No."

"We're down to about ten miles per hour. Think you can make it?"

She looked at him with an open, vulnerable expression he'd never seen before. "Mister, after what I've been through, jumping off a train is a piece of cake."

"Listen..." He knelt and put his hands on her arms. "I'm sorry... about... what happened... with the..."

"Shove it, Shockley." She smiled up at him. "Bygones are bygones. I'm okay."

He smiled back, and helped her to her feet. Her legs were weak and rubbery beneath her, and though she tried to conceal the fact, he could see that she was hurting.

"The important thing is not to tense up," he said. "Try to land with your muscles relaxed and roll with your momentum. Duck your shoulders and try to be a ball. That way you stand a good chance of not breaking—"

"Hey, Ben, I learned that stuff in grade school." She smiled warmly. "Don't worry."

"I'll follow you out."

"You're all heart, Shockley. Let's just get the damn thing over with, okay?"

They stood at the door. The hot desert air was rich with the scent of impending rain. Tire clouds were heavy and dark; the sand swirled in miniature tornadoes in the electric breeze.

She turned to him. "Listen, in case I klutz this up and break my neck or something, I... aw, the hell with it."

And she was gone—out the door, tumbling down the sandy roadbed that ran up to the tracks. As Shockley followed her into space, it flashed through his mind how fragile she had suddenly become.

And how indestructible.

He hit the incline feet-first and went into an awkward somersault, then rolled for several yards until he thudded to a halt against a half-buried boulder.

Other than the minor pain in his left hip where he'd hit the rock, he was reasonably sure everything was intact. He stumbled off to his right toward the prone figure of Mally, lying motionless in the dirt.

He knelt and took her wrist to feel for a pulse. At first he felt nothing, and a bolt of panic shot through him. He adjusted his fingers. Then he felt the steady throb of life beneath his index finger.

Cradling her head in his lap, he brushed a few strands of hair from her eyes and ran his fingertips lightly across her face.

Jesus, he thought over and over again. *Jesus. Please be all right. I want you with me, Mally.*

She opened her eyes. "Hey, Shockley. I didn't know you cared."

Josie sat in the precinct lunchroom, a barren, cheerless, hundred and twenty square feet—four faded green walls, three coin-guzzling vending machines, and a long table surrounded by cheap plastic chairs.

Josie was alone, nursing a chocolate bar and a heavily sugared cup of coffee, not giving a damn about the paper work that was piling up back at his desk.

Everything was of minor importance compared to his main, private concern: What was he going to do about Ben?

Or, even more to the point, what was he going to do about Blakelock?

Ever since he'd picked up the phone and heard Ben's voice on the other end of the line, Josie had been right in the middle of the goddamest dilemma of his career.

Of his life.

There wasn't anything he wouldn't do for his friend and partner, Ben Shockley. If only he could get together with him, talk to him, get all the facts, work something out. He was used to working things out together with Ben. But now he was isolated. He was used to depending upon Ben's brains for analyzing the problem. After that they would go after it together, solve it, with Josie using his street smarts to keep them alive.

But this was different, so different. Ben was using his own street smarts to stay alive; he was depending on Josie to be the brains, to figure out what to do.

Christ, he wished he were back on the bricks. Decisions were easier out there. You made them on the spot and lived —or died—with them. Now that he'd been given plenty of opportunity to think, he was finding it a deceptive luxury.

Josie bit into the candy bar without tasting it and washed it down with some coffee. He knew all the while that he was just stalling, eating and drinking without hunger or thirst.

He could feed his face all day and that wasn't going to make his decision any easier.

But he had to make *some* decision, and it would be his alone. He couldn't run it through Ben, like the old days, for an opinion. He had to make a decision, and it would be one that would determine whether Ben Shockley lived or died.

Ben was out there somewhere trying to stay alive. As for the witness, whoever she was, Josie couldn't care less, and he frankly admitted it to himself. They could waste a truckload of witnesses, as far as he was concerned. What good were witnesses these days, anyway? Hell, you could have the Mormon Tabernacle Choir witness a crime, and by the time the judge and the attorneys and the D.A. wrapped up their games, all you got for your trouble was the privilege of watching the defendant do a freedom dance down the court house steps and then thumb his nose at you.

No, Josie's only concern was Ben, and it extended far beyond the simple problem of a fellow cop being in jeopardy. It extended even beyond the limits of a friendship forged over a period of fifteen years. There was a bond of brotherhood between the two of them. This was something Josie had never consciously thought about, but the truth of it was clear, and now he felt the full weight of his responsibility.

And his responsibility went beyond their friendship and

their brotherhood. It rose from the very basis for their relationship—their jobs. Their department. Their livelihoods.

They had been risking their lives for fifteen years, together, for their jobs and their department.

Ben had implied that the two of them would have to stand against the very heart of the department.

The ultimate question now was: What about Blakelock?

How could he go about bringing Ben in without mentioning Blakelock?

It wasn't that he was afraid of Blakelock. It was a question of priorities. His first job was to get Ben in safely.

He couldn't. There was no way. Josie slammed the side of his meaty fist against the table top, then looked quickly around and was relieved that nobody had seen him do it.

Dammit! Who could he talk to? Who would even begin to take him seriously when he said that the most powerful man on the force next to the Chief himself was trying to snuff a witness who could tie him to the mob, and also the detective who'd been sent to bring her in?

Even he himself found it hard to believe. Except for one thing: the information had come from Ben, and that meant it was first-class goods.

Ben was thorough to the point of aggravation. He was a straight-line cop who refused to be fooled by footwork, to whom the easy way out meant nothing more than a shortcut to an erroneous conclusion. If Ben said the President of the United States was out to fry his ass, that was good enough for Josie. In fact, it would have made things a hell of a lot easier if that had been what Ben *had* said. At least that way, Josie thought, he could go to his superiors with something that wasn't a threat to the security of their own jobs.

Josie stuffed the rest of the candy bar into his mouth and tossed the crumpled paper wrapper into a wastebasket.

Pick someone, dammit! He railed at himself for his indecision. *Pick someone you can trust and tell him your story!*

But who? Who's not going to look at you like you just fell out of the sky? Name one cop who... An idea wedged its way into the vicious circle of Josie's thoughts, and he toyed with it, exploring its dimensions, its possibilities, its pitfalls.

There were risks, but they were minimal—at least, as minimal as anything could be under the circumstances. And it was a hell of a lot better than parading up to another cop and announcing that the head of Internal Affairs was joined at the hip with the mob.

Josie finished his coffee, and as the sugary liquid slid down his throat, he began to feel, for the first time since he'd received Ben's call, that he was in control.

The metal shingle hanging outside bore the familiar silhouette of the speeding race-dog and the lettering:

<u>GREYHOUND BUS LINES</u>
<u>Kingman, Arizona</u>

Mally sat on the depot's weatherbeaten steps, watching the sign swing freely in the strong desert wind. In the ladies' room, she'd combed her hair and washed the dust and dirt from her face. But no cleansing could erase the effects of her journey, which had etched its lines around her mouth and eyes.

The glass door behind her swung open, and she turned as Shockley came out and stood beside her.

"The next bus is at two-thirty," he said.

She looked up at him. "It's insane," she said softly. "The whole idea's insane."

"Maybe." He stared off into the distance for a moment, then went back inside, where he approached the clerk. "You're sure that's an express bus?"

"Of course. We don't get all that many buses here. You want a ticket?"

"Not now, thank you."

He went back out to Mally. He held out his hand; she took it and stood up. The wind buffeted their tired bodies. His plan seemed to have revived his spirits, but the craziness of it made Mally feel even weaker.

A clap of thunder in the near distance promised an approaching storm. Mally shivered.

They left the bus depot and walked slowly down the road toward a sterile, brick-fronted motel.

CHAPTER 22

Shockley swung the door shut and slid the deadbolt into place.

The room was as soulless and sterile as the inside of a Band-Aid box. But at least, Ben thought, it was clean, and just now that seemed like a super-luxury.

Gray, clouded light filtered in from the window and cast leaden shadows across the king-sized bed. A faded velvet canopy dangled from the mottled acoustical ceiling in a pathetic semblance of elegance. The door to the bathroom stood open exposing a wall of imitation marble in a garish shade of pink.

Ben slumped into an orange leatherette armchair and let his head fall back. "Go ahead"—he waved toward the bath room—"you first."

"Okay, I won't argue with you," Mally crossed the room, pausing at the bathroom door. "Hey," she said, with an exhausted smile. "This time I promise to come back." She went in and shut the door.

Ben heard the sound of running water. He got up from the chair and sat down on the edge of the bed. The sound of the water was comforting, and he enjoyed the anticipation of his own bath.

"Hey, Mally?" he called as he reached for the phone on the nightstand.

She opened the door and peeked out.

"I'll get us something to eat. What'll you have?"

"Surprise me."

They held each other's eyes for the briefest of moments, sharing the bond of their past and the uncertainty of their future. Then Mally stepped back into the pink cavern and closed the door.

Ben picked up the receiver, his finger poised over the single digit that would summon room service, his mouth already watering with the thought of their first meal in God knows how long.

But there was something else he had to get out of the way first. He dialed the number for the Phoenix P.D.

Josie snatched up his phone with an impatient frown, figuring it was somebody asking for this or that piece of paperwork that he hadn't got to yet. "Detective Josephson here."

"It's me."

"Ben?" He cupped his hand around the mouthpiece and glanced around the detective squad room to make sure that everybody was occupied with other matters. Then he spoke in a hushed tone. "You okay?"

"Listen to me, Josie. I'm coming in."

"Coming in? Coming in *where?*"

"City Hall."

"Ben, for chrissake, that's nuts!"

"Write this down—"

"Jesus, Ben, you can't. Not that way. I've got something in the works. Something that can save you."

"Please, Josie, just get a pencil." Shockley's voice was a

frazzled whisper, and Josie found himself obediently holding a pencil between his thick fingers.

"Okay, okay, Ben, I'm ready, but—"

"Mesa off-ramp. Up Central Avenue. Down Adams. Straight to City Hall. You copy that?"

Josie scribbled the directions on a scratch pad. "Yeah, yeah, I got it: Mesa ramp, Central, Adams, City Hall."

"Right. Five minutes after I leave here," Ben said calmly, "Blakelock's gonna hear I'm coming, so—"

"How's he gonna know?"

"He'll know, believe me. I know he'll try to stop me, so give him that route."

"Give it to him? What the hell—"

"I want him to know exactly where I'll be traveling. Tell him to clear the streets. This is between him and me. I don't want any innocent people caught in the middle."

"Ben, this is crazy!"

Josie had to fight to keep his voice down. He glanced around again at his co-workers; they were all still busy.

"Crazy," he said more softly.

"And give him this message for me," Shockley said. "Tell him I know why he picked me for the job. Tell him he was wrong. Tell him I'm coming for him. Tell him I'm gonna nail his ass to the wall. You hear me?"

"Jesus!"

"And to protect yourself, Josie, tell him you think I've flipped, gone completely wacko. He'll know I haven't, but at least he won't think you're trying to help me."

"Christ, Ben, he'll have every cop on the force out there! Play it my way. Please!"

"Like I said, I'm coming in."

There was a click, and then the steady buzz of the dial tone.

Josie stared at the notes on his scratch pad. Ben had said to give those directions to Blakelock, and that's what he'd do.

But if that got Ben killed, he'd never forgive himself.

Ben held the button down for several seconds, playing back the conversation in his mind. He'd just committed two lives to almost certain disaster. That's what the odds said.

But then the odds also said that he and Mally should have been cold meat for several hours already. And they were still alive. Battered, aching, emotionally frayed to the breaking point, but still alive. Alive and ready to make the plunge—the plunge he dared hope wouldn't be the final one for both of them.

Alive. And hungry. Ben released the button on the phone and dialed for room service.

"Room service? Yeah, this is three-fourteen. Send up some food. Two steaks, rare. Baked potato. Salad. Whatever comes with them. And a bottle of good red wine."

He waited while the order was repeated for his confirmation.

"Anything else, sir?" room service asked.

"Yeah. Do you have a gift shop?"

CHAPTER 23

The rain slanted against their window. Lightning flashed in across their table and their faces, as the storm drenched the desert.

Refreshed from their baths, their hunger slaked by the juicy steaks, their clothes cleaned and pressed by the motel's valet, they felt again what it was like to be human beings.

Comfort permeated their bodies and buoyed their spirits.

Relaxed, they dawdled over the last of their wine, neither wanting the pleasant interlude to end.

The light of the single candle played across Mally's face.

She had applied lipstick and a bit of mascara, and her eyes glowed in the light. Her hair was brushed and hung softly over her shoulders.

"Enjoy your dinner?" she asked.

Ben glanced at his plate, empty save for the meticulously cleaned T-bone that angled across it. "It was a second-rate steak," he said bluntly.

Then a satisfied smile spread across his face. "It was also the best meal of my life."

Mally sipped her wine. "I'd be interested to hear about it —your life."

"My life? Shit. You already know most of it, what I do for a living."

"I mean the rest of it—before, how you grew up, every thing."

"Is this the spot where my tenth-grade teacher walks through the door and surprises me?"

"I'll bet he had his hands full, if the rest of the class was anything like you."

"She. I had a crush on her. I set her desk on fire once. Her papers. Yeah, she had her hands full. As a matter of fact, we were all a bunch of punk-faced delinquents."

"That I can believe. Rolling drunks and stomping queers, right?"

"No, we saved our hostility mainly for each other—it was safer that way." Ben drained his glass and Mally refilled it, emptying the bottle. "Hey, keep some for yourself," he said.

"I ordered another, while you were taking your bath. You don't mind?"

"No. Good. We'll get shit-faced here, then stagger into some police station like a couple of drunks ready for the tank."

"Not on a couple of bottles of wine, after a good meal. Our nerves have earned it."

"I think my nerves retired. They're on pension."

"So..." She put her chin in her hands and looked at him. "You were fighters, huh?"

"Yeah. At least we thought we were."

"So how does it happen? How does a punk-faced delinquent wind up changing sides?"

There was a knock at the door. Ben opened it, took the wine from the waiter, signed the check, and returned. He opened the wine and filled their glasses. He sat staring into the brilliant red wine in his glass, helped by the reflection of the candle in the clear stem.

"Tell me," she said.

"Okay."

He had never talked about his childhood to anyone, not even Josie. It wasn't that he was ashamed of it; it was simply the past, and for Ben that was reason enough to bury it. The only glory in his past had been his glorious dreams for the future. And when the future turned out to be a mockery of his dreams, he put the past out of his mind.

By the rhythm of the rain, cooling and calming, the warmth of the wine, the courage of the woman who sat across from him, the unexpected ease of their conversation, the intimacy they had developed going through a series of hells together—everything combined to tell him this was a person he could talk to, a person he *should* talk to, a person who would listen without making judgments.

And so he told her.

When Ben Shockley was a kid, in Chicago, he hated cops.

So did his friend Mike.

"Fuckin' cops!" said Mike as they emerged one Saturday afternoon from the Liberty Theater, flushed with thrilling memories of the heroic Silver Eagles, the combat flyers whose exploits were a regular feature of the Liberty's war time newsreels.

Mike had addressed his comment in the direction of a distant corner where two cops stood quietly conversing. It had no basis in experience, but such comments were heard often from older boys in the decaying neighborhood. It seemed a good, tough remark to make.

"Yeah, fuckers," Ben said.

They went around the side of a building, noisily knocked over some garbage cans, and ran, delighted in their exploit.

There were a number of gangs of pre-teenage boys in the area. They were not so much dangerous as threatening, but independents like Ben and Mike were at a disadvantage.

So, with pals, they formed the Silver Eagles as a kind of self-protection. A dozen of them signed oaths in blood from their pricked fingers, obliging them to be loyal for the rest of their lives, to lay down their lives without question to save one another, and to contribute a quarter a week to the "defense fund" (which paid, at first, for candy and cigarettes).

They carried no guns in those days—none of the younger gangs did. They couldn't afford them, the Silver Eagles decided, until the defense fund had been built up. So they carried sticks, sawed-off broom handles, small pocket knives, and, later, bicycle chains.

Fights with other gangs were common and, though not lethal, extremely painful.

"Jesus," Mike said, after a confrontation in which they had been routed by the Windy City Warriors, "I think I got busted ribs. That one guy had a pipe."

"Lemme see," Ben said, filled with curiosity. This would be the most serious injury one of them had yet suffered.

"Cops!" bellowed one of the gang.

Three cops trotted around the corner toward them, swinging their nightsticks. "Hold it right there, boys!"

They ran. But the cops were faster. The boys were corraled and thrown roughly against a building wall.

"We'll take all the sticks and knives, everything," one cop said, holding his billy across Ben's chest.

Ben glanced around at his buddies, heard their heavy breathing, felt their dependence on him. "Bullshit," he said.

"Now, now," the cop said, feeling his pockets and extracting a knife, "you wouldn't want me to tell your father about how you mouthed off to the police?"

"I ain't got no father." He heard the rattle of weapons being confiscated from other gang members.

"Is that so?" The cop was a beer-bellied, red-haired Irishman named Dougan, whom they usually saw on the beat. He had a grin wide enough to drive a truck through. He usually worked the beat alone, except when there was a rumble.

"It's the truth. He's..." Ben couldn't bring himself to say it. He was still unable to face squarely the truth that his father was dead, that he'd put a bullet through his own head and been buried in the ground, taking his own dreams with him, and some of Ben's as well.

"I'm sorry to hear that," the cop said, releasing his hold on Ben. "But I'm gonna tell you this: whether you got an old man or not, I ain't lettin' you run wild on *my* beat. I've got my eye on you—*all* of you kids."

"My buddy's got busted ribs."

"No, I ain't!" Mike glared daggers at Ben. "I ain't got nothin'. Can't nobody hurt me!"

The cop looked back and forth between them.

Ben felt Mike's courageous denial burn through him. "It was another guy got hurt, guy that got away," he said embarrassed.

"I'll tell you boys something," the cop said. "I'm gonna let you go this time. But there's big trouble for you up the line, if you keep this up. Trouble with *me.* And I can handle it, don't kid yourselves. Now, *scram.*"

He waved his stick and the gang scampered off in different directions. Except for Mike and Ben, who ran together.

"Fuckin' cops," Mike muttered when they finally stopped to catch their breath.

"That asshole better not mess with me," Ben said. "When we get our guns, I'll personally blow his head off."

"We'll get 'em all," Mike said, "one at a time."

There were more gang fights, more confrontations with the police. Sometimes Ben and others were taken to the station house, where the riot act was read to them, and they were threatened with jail. More often they were taken home, mortified, to be presented to their parents by the policeman.

"What am I gonna do with you?" Ben's mother would say, shaking her prematurely gray head and putting her red-veined hand over her breast. "Ever since your father..." She could never say the words either. She would cry and order him to bed, and more than once she sat up all night long until she had to leave in the morning for the dry-cleaners where she had a job as a presser.

He had little to do with his mother. He saw her as little as possible, and spoke to her only when he had to. He loved her, but she was only sadness to him. He made her sad with his behavior; she made him sad with her weariness and her work and her hopelessness.

Those nights when she didn't sit up, Ben would sneak out, meet Mike, and they would go over the latest events that had got them in trouble.

School was not much better. Ben and Mike went to school simply because that was where their friends were, where the girls were—and that's where the action was, during the day.

The teachers had virtually given up hope of controlling them, and counted the minutes to the end of the classes just as anxiously as the boys did.

Miss Owens was an English teacher. The game with her was to make farting noises that drove her crazy; there was the joy of ogling her sharp breasts when she leaned forward and her long legs when she bent over. Ben's fantasies were unsophisticated. But more than once he got an erection just from looking at her and had to leave at the end of the class with his books held over his crotch.

Miss Owens was haughty and aloof. She was a challenge.

And so while the other boys contented themselves with ogling and making their farting noises, Ben made a plan. He snuck in one day and set the top of her desk afire, turning their most recent test papers into a pile of ashes and Miss Owens into a frenzied, screaming hag.

He'd got to her, all right. And he was a hero. The class never had to take the test over.

In time, things grew more serious. A few girls started hanging around. One was named Martha.

"She's beggin' for it," Mike said to Ben one night, watching Martha wriggle her tight ass on the lap of another gang member.

"Yeah," Ben said.

The next night Mike brought a bottle of muscatel to the gathering. He passed it around. "I need me a broad," he said.

When Martha dropped in, half the gang members were high—partly from drinking the wine, partly from *knowing* they had been drinking wine.

Mike pulled her down on his lap. "You been beggin' for it," he said. She looked a little scared. Mike began kissing her and caressing her—right there in front of everybody.

Another boy went over and started kissing her, and then another went. All of a sudden they were ripping Martha's clothes off. They threw her on the floor. They pinned her arms and legs. Mike was the first one on top of her...

Ben ran. That wasn't how he wanted it. He had imagined something more pleasant, more sweet, more private. He didn't remember if Martha had screamed or not, if she had said anything at all. Maybe she was begging for it, like Mike said. Maybe it was okay. But it was not how Ben wanted it.

Should he have done something to stop it? He didn't want to see it.

He ran until he couldn't run anymore, and then sat down on the curb. He began to think. He thought of Martha's firm, small, white breasts; they had been exposed when the guys pulled off her blouse and bra. Maybe she was begging for it. He almost wished he had stayed.

His turn came not long after. He was standing outside the English classroom, waiting to go in, when Wendy sidled up, leaned against the wall, and looked at him. She wore heavy eye makeup and bright red lipstick and sheer blouses that you could see her black bras under.

"Let's cut," she said.

"Naw." He had been thinking about Miss Owens, about her breasts and legs, and was looking forward to ogling her in class. He had dreamed about her the night before—a dream so embarrassing that he would never mention it, not even to Mike.

"Scared?" Wendy looked at him with half-closed eyes.

"Course not."

"Rather look at Miss Owens than me?"

"Course not. Just that"—he shuffled his feet nervously—"what would we do?"

"Go someplace. Your mother working?"

"Yeah."

"Go to your place. Mess around."

"What do you mean?"

"We'll play cards," she said, taking his elbow and steering him towards the stairs. "We'll play Go Fish."

They left the school. Ben really believed she wanted to play cards, but as soon as they got to his house and closed the door, Wendy put her arms around his neck and kissed him.

He kissed her back. She ran her hands up and down his sides; he did the same to her.

"Oh, you make me dizzy," she said, pushing him back and staggering a couple of steps. "I gotta lie down. Take me to a bed."

He took her into his bedroom and watched her flop down on the bed.

"Kiss me," she said.

He bent over and kissed her. She pulled him down on top of her. She squirmed her body against his. He got an enormous erection and began to lose his breath. Feeling that he was going crazy, he grabbed her.

"Not so fast, buster," she said suddenly, pushing him off. "You better cool down."

Wendy got off the bed and went into the bathroom.

He tried to cool down. He rummaged through his dresser drawer and found a deck of cards. He figured they'd better play Go Fish.

When she came back, she was wearing only pink panties and her black bra. "You've got too many clothes on," she said. "I'll help you."

He stood dumbfounded, his head reeling, as she took off his shirt and pants. He closed his eyes. He hurt. He was suffering what they called "blue balls."

Wendy pushed him down on the bed and crawled on top of him.

"Take me," she said.

"Where?"

"Stick it in me, for chrissake!" She slithered out of her panties and pulled his jockey shorts down.

He fumbled frantically for proper placement. He couldn't find it. She could.

And that was his first.

They lay side by side, sweating, their breath easing.

"Now you'll have to marry me," she said.

"Why?"

"'Cause I'm pregnant."

Eventually she was, though not by him. Somebody else took her hurriedly to the altar. But there elapsed several weeks during which Ben's pride at having scored was outweighed by his terror of the possible consequences of not having taken what Wendy called "precautions."

From then on he did. But he found casual sex unsatisfying —he wanted somebody to be close to, to talk to. Other gang members were pairing off with steady girlfriends. Ben didn't.

It seemed that every time he was with a girl he liked, the

more he wanted to talk, the less he could. He couldn't share himself.

The neighborhood was getting meaner. Fights were rougher. Mike was shot in the arm by a zip gun and taken to hospital. The rest of the gang was hauled into the station house and thrown into a cell for an hour. But they weren't booked.

When Ben left the station, the Irish cop, Dougan, came up to him on the steps.

"You're heading for an early coffin, Shockley," he said. "I don't wanna be the one to put you there. Think about your old man. Maybe he's watching you. How would you feel about that?"

Ben cried that night, after his mother had gone to bed. He didn't really know why. He just felt alone.

The next day he visited Mike at the hospital.

"Fuckin" cops," Mike said. His eyes were proud.

"Cops didn't shoot you," Ben said.

"Cops brought me to this stinkin' shit-hole. I didn't need no hospital. Shit."

Ben admired him.

"We're movin'," Mike said. "My pa says we're gettin' outta this neighborhood. He says it ain't worth it. Other side of town. Shit. Have to start all over. I'll check out the action. When I know what's workin', I'll send for you. We can set up over there."

He never heard from Mike again.

The gang stayed pretty much to itself. Everybody was upset over what had happened to Mike. Squabbles broke out. Some members wanted to make guns and use them.

Others, including Ben, wanted to cool it for a while.

Ben's faction wanted him to be president. The others wanted a guy called "Toad." Toad had scars around his eyes from street fights, and a broken nose from Golden Gloves.

Ben's group was standing on a street corner one night, talking things over, when Toad and his bunch came up.

Toad took his hand slowly out of his pocket. He had a zip gun. "This is what a real president has," he said.

"Put it away," Ben said.

"Scared?"

"No?

"Then why don't you put it away for me, Shockley?"

War began. Everybody was punching and kicking. Boys went down, got up, went down again. Blood flowed from noses and mouths.

Ben and Toad were trying to choke each other. They wrestled apart, and Ben caught a looping right on his ear.

Ben snapped Toad's nose with a straight right, then heaved a mighty roundhouse left that dropped his enemy to the sidewalk.

Suddenly Dougan, the cop, strode into the melee, bouncing boys left and right off his big belly. The fighting stopped.

Boys lay on the sidewalk; others were kneeling or standing.

They all stared at Dougan.

Dougan grinned. He grabbed Ben by the T-shirt. "I saw that punch, Shockley. That's not fighting. That's no way to throw a left hook. It has to be shorter, tighter. *This* is a left hook!"

All at once Ben was lying on his back on the sidewalk, looking up at Dougan. The punch echoed in his head, and his jawbone was numb.

"That was a left hook, boys," Dougan said. "I got other punches, too. Anybody wanna see 'em?"

The boys backed off.

"Next time I see a bunch of you punks together around here, I'm gonna show you some of my other punches. You got that? Now *scram!*"

The gangs took off.

"Let me help you up." Smiling his broad smile, Dougan leaned over and stuck out his hand. He pulled Ben up, patted his rump, and held up his big fist. "I could throw left hooks all day," he said, grinning. "And I never lost a fistfight in my life. Now, you scram, too."

When Ben got home, he found a small card stuck in his back pocket. The message said, "Call me—Dougan," and gave a telephone number.

Ben called.

"The reason I belted you, Shockley," Dougan said, "was because, believe it or not, I like you. You might turn out okay. I like the other guys, too, but for some reason I've picked you for special treatment. You got a job to do, to straighten yourself out. But I think you can do it. I think you can do any job you set your mind to. I belted you because I wanted to remind you that right now you're still a punk. You and the other guys, all punks. I knew your father, Shockley. That surprise you? Hell, I know everybody in this neighborhood. He wasn't a punk. Maybe I punched you because he wasn't around to do it. Think about it. We may not talk about it again."

The gang split up. Ben finished high school and knocked around different jobs. He got work in a supermarket, then was laid off; he got work in construction, and was laid off there, too.

Then his mother lost her job. They said she was sick.

She and Ben moved to Phoenix, for the climate. Ben got work on a tree farm. A couple of years later, his mother died.

He took her body to Sioux City for burial, then went back to Chicago to clean up a few legal matters. There were some aunts and uncles he had hardly ever seen who wanted to make sure that Ben's mother hadn't had some little savings account somewhere that maybe they could get their hands on.

He wandered around his old neighborhood. It was changed. Buildings were gone. There was more garbage.

People more sullen.

There was a new cop there, young, with a hatchet face.

Ben asked about Dougan. "I knew him when I lived here," he said. "Did he retire?"

"No. Wish he had. They killed him."

"Killed, him?"

"One day he just didn't show up on the beat. He was off duty the night before. Around midnight he saw a couple of guys breaking into a liquor store. So he got out of his car—he wasn't even in uniform—and tried to stop them. One of the guys pulled a gun and shot him, then they took off.

"They found him the next morning. He was dead, lying at the bottom of the steps to County General Hospital. There was a trail of blood stretching back to the liquor store, three blocks away. Dougan had been shot in both legs, took another slug in the neck, and two in his belly. They figured it must have taken him at least forty-five minutes to crawl from the liquor store to the hospital. Forty-five minutes, and no one stopped to help."

The cop spat into the gutter. "This place ain't like you left it."

"Dead." Ben stared off.

"Were you a friend of his?"

Ben looked at him. "He was a friend. I was a punk, just a punk."

The cop nodded. "Yeah. So were they. The guys that shot him. I said nobody stopped to help—I don't know if that's true. Maybe nobody even saw Dougan crawling along. But the way things are around here now, people are scared to help a cop. Anyway, he was dead. Three nights later the same two guys knocked over another liquor store and got caught. Me and my partner had it staked out. They admitted shooting Dougan. They knew him. Shit, one of them Dougan had even brought around to the precinct a couple times, talked to him, tried to straighten him out. They were punks, just punks. Maybe they won't be when they get out. But that don't help Dougan any."

"No. I'm sorry."

The cop stared at him. "So how about you? You look like you straightened yourself out okay."

"Yeah. I'm okay. I wish I could tell Dougan that he got the job done."

"The job?"

"He'd know what I meant."

The candle burned low, flickering and spitting as the wick sank gradually into the little pool of melted wax. Ben studied his wineglass. He glanced up at Mally.

"So then I came back to Phoenix, and one thing led to another, and eventually I felt myself drawn to the police department. I didn't have a record or anything, so I figured I could get a job. The city was growing. They were hiring cops. And by then, see, naturally I had figured out what cops were all about Hell, they had never been after me. They were just doing their jobs, just trying to feed their kids. They were the law. I broke the law several times, and I could have been booked—should have been, maybe. But I was lucky."

He smiled at Mally. "By that time, cops were the ones I respected most. They were the only people I ever knew who really stood for something,"

He turned his wineglass slowly. "So as soon as I could I joined the force. Pay wasn't a lot—still isn't, for that matter. But I was so goddam proud. Uniform, badge, gun. Guys working with you, sharing your job, helping each other out. I really had a thing about the law. I was going to be one hell of a cop. I worked hard, studied the manual, studied all kinds of books about police work."

Ben sighed. "I advanced pretty good for a while. But then, up the line, you could see you had to get involved in things like office politics and ass-kissing. I couldn't handle that. I just wanted to be good at my work. I dreamed of the big case that was going to come. The one I'd break wide open and earn my captain's stripes with. I guess every rookie feels the same way. Well, I felt that way even when I *wasn't* a rookie any more. I was going to climb the ladder by my work alone."

Mally nodded. "I think you were doing the right—"

He held up his hand. "And there was another dream that went along with it. A dream that I'd marry a woman I loved, a woman who'd love me... we'd have a family... kids... a home... all the dumb things people take for granted. Normal things. Things I never had when I was growing up. But I guess... I guess I just thought about my work."

"We all need our dreams, Ben." Mally blinked a few times. "Otherwise things get very lonely. I know. I've been there."

"That makes two of us, then. Because the years just drifted by, and somewhere, sometime—I couldn't even tell you when—there was no more dream. Just a job. Hours to put in. Years to count off. I watched other men break the big cases. Saw them getting married, having kids. And I was still there. On the bricks."

He concentrated on the delicate, full-blown beauty of the white roses he had bought from the gift shop. "It was like standing on the other side of a glass wall and watching the world go by."

Mally reached out and laid her hand gently on his, a gesture that he accepted without surprise. Then he got up abruptly from the table and went to the window. He stood staring out at the pounding storm.

"Quite a tale of progress, isn't it?" He did not turn to face her. "Instead of breaking the big case, I get picked to go down with it. That oughta be an inspiration to a lot of punks growing up."

Mally watched him light a cigarette, and smiled to herself.

Her cop had finally emerged from behind the diamond-hard veneer. She was impressed and moved not so much by the story he had told as by the fact that he had been able to tell it to her. She wondered if he had ever told it before, and she decided he probably hadn't. Maybe to another woman. But it wouldn't have been exactly the same. Nobody would have *heard* it exactly the same way she had. She was saddened that her involvement made such a sorry climax to the story.

"To hell with them," she said at last. "You don't have to do it. Neither of us does. Nobody's making us go back—not any more. We can go to Mexico, Canada, anywhere. Anywhere in the world."

"Sure." His back was still turned. "And live like kings."

"I've got money." She grinned at him. "I've got five thousand dollars in Vegas."

"Put it on a horse. Why don't you put it on Mally-No-Show and make a bundle?"

"We could live okay, for a while, on my five thousand."

He turned now to face her, exhaling a filmy cloud of cigarette smoke. "And what happens when the money runs out?"

"Okay, then let's spend it here," Mally said. "Let's use it to buy a pickup truck, an old car, something unobtrusive. We can take the back roads, turn ourselves in at a precinct. Anything but City Hall. We'll ask for protective custody, talk to the D.A.—"

"That's exactly what I want you to do," he interrupted.

"What do you mean?"

"I want you to turn yourself in, all that."

She fixed him with a look, afraid of the answer to the question she had to ask. "How about you?"

"I'm going in," he said simply.

"Why?"

He moved back to the window. "We both know why

Blakelock picked me. He thought I would be an easy mark, a quick hit, somebody who'd never be missed. I have to prove he was wrong. I have to prove I'm a better cop than he thought."

"So you're going to do that?"

"Yup."

"Then I'm going with you."

He spun toward her. "No, you're not! As of now, you're free. You're not my prisoner anymore. Take off. Disappear."

"Don't hold your breath."

"Look, this is between me and Blakelock."

"Since when, mister? Since when? Since when wasn't I involved in this? Since when wasn't my life in just as much danger as yours? Since when wasn't I part of Blakelock's set up?"

"I just meant…" He took a deep breath. "I mean that what I have to do, my plan for getting to him, only needs me. You'll be better off splitting. I can take care of it from here on."

"Christ, Ben, you said yourself you didn't think it would work! Listen to your own conclusions, for God's sake."

"At least this way someone will know I tried."

"Who? Blakelock?"

"No. Me."

Mally started to say something, then shook her head. She pushed her chair angrily back from the table and crossed the room to the phone. Ben turned back to the storm, drumming his fingers on the window sill, dimly aware of her voice asking for a long-distance number. He waited, then heard her speak.

"Mom, Hi, it's me."

Frowning at the words, he kept his eyes on the window as though concerned with the flooding landscape.

"I'm fine, Mom." She held up her free hand, as if to stem the flow of her mother's words. "Sure I'm sure. I wouldn't lie to you. How's Daddy? ...Jesus, Mom, he's been complaining about that for as long as I can remember. He ought to see a specialist, not that quack he goes to." She gave a little sigh of annoyance. "Yeah, okay, that's just my opinion... What? No, I quit that job. I didn't want to be a secretary for the rest of my fife."

Her eyes held on Shockley as he moved to the table and stubbed out his cigarette.

"Listen, Mom," she said. "I've got some big news. I'm in love."

Ben almost pushed the ashtray through the table, then stared in disbelief at her gloating, triumphant smile. Her voice seemed to him to be coming from the far end of a long tunnel.

"...Shockley," she was saying, "Ben Shockley... Mom, what difference does it make what church he goes to? We love each other. We're going to get married. We're going to live in Arizona and settle down and have kids... Yeah, I'm in Kingman right now... Kingman Arizona. It's a little town about halfway between Las Vegas and Phoenix... Yeah, he's got a job in Phoenix... Look, we don't have to talk about everything now. So just be happy for us, okay? ...Well, we really haven't decided yet. Maybe up in northern Arizona, near the canyon. You can still buy land up there without going bankrupt, and it's supposed to be beautiful."

Ben stared at her as she smiled and nodded.

"When? Oh, we have some business to clear up first, both of us, in Phoenix. But that really shouldn't take too long... Jesus, Mom, I don't *feel* like inviting three dozen people. I just wanted you to know, that's all... That's right, Mom, just like it sounds. S-H-O-C-K-L-E-Y. Okay, Mom, I gotta hang up now. Tell Daddy for me, will you? Love you. Bye."

She hung up and immediately dialed another number.

Ben could no longer keep silent. "Somewhere near the

canyon, huh?" He meant for it to sound sarcastic, but somehow it didn't. It sounded unsettlingly serious.

"Congratulations, you got good ears," Mally told him, and then turned her attention to the new call. "Bernie? It's Mally. You still got a line on that horse, Mally-No-Show? ...Yeah? What's the line now? ... A hundred to one? Dynamite! I want five thousand dollars' worth... Yeah, I know we got the same name. That's why I feel something special about her... That's right. Don't hassle me, Bernie, you know I'm good for it. Okay? And Bernie, put it on the nose. She's going to be a winner!"

Mally's confidence was emphasized by the way she banged down the receiver. Then, ignoring Shockley's puzzled gaze, she strode to the table and removed the roses from the vase.

Shaking the moisture from the stems, she gently replaced the roses in their box, tucked the box under her arm, and looked Ben squarely in the eyes.

"Okay, mister, let's go," she said.

CHAPTER 24

Airbrakes hissing, the giant Scenicruiser groaned to a stop in front of the bus depot. Levering the door open with habitual nonchalance, the driver waited patiently as his passengers began to disembark into the raging storm. He nodded sympathetically at their complaints about the depot's lack of a covered walkway, then checked his motor gauges.

At the rear, the last few passengers collected their belongings from their seats.

Shockley stepped briskly up to the bus door. "Lift those hands, fella, nice and easy." Standing in the rain, he kept his Magnum trained steadily on the driver. "I said lift them. Now let's see it."

The driver whipped around, mouth agape, eyes wide.

"What the hell you doing?" he gasped.

"Just what it looks like I'm doing," Ben said calmly.

"But… but… this is an official Greyhound bus!"

"I don't give a shit if it's the *Queen Elizabeth.* Take your hands off the door lever."

"What're you gonna do, mister?"

"You'll see. Lift 'em."

His lips trembling, the driver slowly raised his hands.

Mally came up beside Ben, and they both climbed aboard the bus.

Handing her his gun, Shockley quickly patted the befuddled driver, checking for weapons.

"I ain't got nothin', mister! I ain't got nothin' on me, honest!"

"I know. Believe me, I'm a pro at this. Just relax, do as you're told."

Still clutching the box of roses under one arm, Mally turned to scan the stunned, frozen faces of the few passengers remaining aboard. She held the gun on them with casual confidence and spoke in the cool, efficient tones of a stewardess.

"We apologize for this temporary inconvenience, ladies and gentlemen, but at this time I'm afraid I'll have to ask you to leave the bus. Please make sure you have all your belongings. I promise you that arrangements will be made for your continued journey as soon as possible."

They stood or sat where they were. They were immobilized with uncertainty, apparently unable to grasp the contradictions of this pretty woman and the huge pistol in her hand.

Mally swung the Magnum suddenly in a flashing arc toward the open door. *"Haul ass!"*

Galvanized into action, they lunged for coats and travel cases in the overhead racks, fought for position in the narrow aisle. The driver was the last to leave the hijacked bus.

Five minutes later, the passengers stood grouped about the driver outside the bus. They huddled forlornly in the rain, water dripping from their noses, their shoulders hunched against the weather and the shock of what had happened.

Suitcases hastily retrieved from the cargo bays stood on the ground behind them.

Ben stood framed in the doorway of the Scenicruiser, looking down at the frightened mass of people. He kept his Magnum on them.

"Like they say on TV"—he raised his voice—"I'll need some volunteers from the audience." He did not smile, but jabbed the gun three times, singling out three men. "You, you, and you. Back inside the bus."

"But he's my *husband*!" A woman, her dark hair plastered to her face by the rain, instinctively grabbed her man's arm. "Please! Don't take him. He's my husband." She whimpered a little.

"And he still will be when I'm through with him," Ben said. "So don't worry. I'm just borrowing him for a little job."

Gently and with dignity, the man removed his wife's hand from his arm and stepped forward with the two others.

The driver cleared his throat. "Give it up, mister," he said.

"You won't get five miles."

"Maybe. Maybe not."

"You're crazy."

"So I've been told," Ben said. "Thanks for the use of your buggy."

He backed up into the bus and waved the hostages inside.

The driver came forward, his mouth opening to speak, but his words were cut off when Mally levered the door shut.

Inside the bus there was silence for a moment, except for the rain pelting noisily against the roof. A blend of fear and curiosity flitted over the features of the three men as they eyed their captors.

"Go back three rows and sit down," Ben ordered, and they did as they were told—two on the left of the aisle, one on the right. "Now," he continued, "any of you familiar with this immediate territory?"

Hesitantly, the man whose wife had tried to hold him back raised his hand. "I live about a mile from here."

"Fine. Then you can show me where..."

. . .

"Your Honor, may counsel approach the bench?"

"Very well."

John Feyderspiel, his pinstriped suit crisp and unwrinkled, his black shoes polished like a mirror, strode confidently forward.

The judge leaned toward the prosecutor. "What is it, Mr. Feyderspiel?"

"I've just received word that I have an urgent message that may have some important bearing on this case, if it's agreeable to the defense, I'd like a ten-minute recess to evaluate the information."

"I see. Why didn't you make this request in open court?"

"Well, sir, I didn't wish to prejudice the jury in the event the information proved to be worthless or inadmissible."

"I see." Well aware of Feyderspiel's reputation for shrewd courtroom maneuvering, the judge turned the request thoughtfully in his mind. Then he beckoned at the table across the room from the prosecutors side. "Defense counsel will please approach the bench."

A paunchy, balding man with a nervous tic at a corner of his mouth came forward from the defense table, his wingtip shoes squeaking.

"Your Honor." He nodded respectfully.

The judge explained Feyderspiel's request, and the defense counsel knitted his brows. "I understand, Your Honor, that Mr. Feyderspiel wishes to recess in order to go out and get more information to help him with his case. But, you see, I came fully prepared to—"

"As I understand it, Mr. Hoffer, it is entirely new information that has just come to the surface." The judge smiled benignly.

"Yes, Your Honor. Of course, if it's valid information, and

admissible, and would help the cause of justice—well, then, I would of course have no—"

"I assure you, Mr. Hoffer, that if the information is not admissible, it will not *be* admitted in this court."

"Well, sometimes... Feyderspiel, you know, he—"

"In the interests of justice, Mr. Hoffer." Feyderspiel was smiling.

"No objection, Your Honor," Defense Attorney Hoffer said resignedly.

The judge banged his gavel. "This court stands in recess until two forty-five."

Feyderspiel turned instantly on his heel and headed briskly for the double doors of the courtroom.

Josie was waiting in the corridor, trying to look casual but unable to conceal his tenseness.

Feyderspiel stood stiffly before him. "You wanted to see me, Detective Josephson?" he asked formally.

Feyderspiel was making no effort to conceal his annoyance at being interrupted in trial of a case. He was the golden boy of the D.A.'s office, a brilliant young attorney who had established himself as a superior prosecutor. It was widely recognized that he was one of those lawyers who get quick, concentrated experience working for the D.A., establish names for themselves, then leave the D.A.'s office for high-paying jobs with a major firm. Flashing annoyance was one of the many ways in which he immediately seized the offensive, whether the circumstance was social or professional. And he had little time for down-at-the-heels detectives.

"You wanted to see me?" Feyderspiel repeated, as Josie hesitated.

"Sorry to bother you, sir, but something's come up."

"I assumed that already, since that was exactly the message I received."

"Yes, sir..."

"Well, let's have it, Josephson. I'm in court. I have a case to prosecute. I'm not in the habit of asking judges for recesses unless it's important."

"Yes, sir. It is..."

Feyderspiel folded his arms.

"It's about Ben Shockley."

"Yes?" Feyderspiel's eyes widened a fraction. He looked intently at Josie.

"He wouldn't even listen to the offer you told me to make him. I don't even know where he was calling from. He didn't tell me anything, except—well, it's like maybe he's flipped, sir, gone completely wacko."

"Except?"

"Except that he said he's coming in. And he said he's gonna nail Blakelock to the wall. I don't know what the hell he was talking about-just kind of raving. He even gave me the exact route he's gonna be using—straight to City Hall!"

Feyderspiel stared at him, arms still folded. He blinked slowly with calculated confidence, then nodded. "You're sure of this?"

"Absolutely, sir. That is, I'm sure what he *said.* I copied down the information myself. He wanted to be sure Commander Blakelock knew exactly what was happening." Josie produced the scribbled notation of Shockley's route and handed it to the prosecutor.

Feyderspiel did not take his eyes off Josie's. "Any idea," he said casually, "why he called you, particularly?"

Josie shrugged. "Just that, I don't know, the way he was talking... maybe just because we been partners for so long, you know."

Feyderspiel nodded.

Josie's expression changed suddenly. "Sir, whatever you may think, whatever you hear, Ben Shockley's a good man. He just wanted Commander Blakelock to know what he said. You're the only guy I know to talk to."

Feyderspiel nodded again, scanned the note quickly, and

slipped it into his coat pocket. He knew that the first thing he had to do was put Josie at ease. He had established his own superiority in the relationship; now gaining the detective's complete confidence was absolutely paramount. That probably wouldn't be a particularly difficult objective to attain, since Josephson was clearly in desperate need of an ally.

And since Detective Josephson was, in Feyderspiel's unerring judgment, telling the truth.

The prosecutor reached out an impeccably manicured hand and gave the upper part of Josie's arm a conspiratorial squeeze. "Your friend's a single-minded man, Josephson. But between the two of us, I think we can save his integrity as well as his life. Do you trust me?"

"Yes."

"And are you with me?"

Josie took a deep breath. "Yes, sir, I'm with you, all the way."

The rotted wooden door gave way with a splintering crash and toppled to the floor, carrying with it a rain-soaked sign announcing that the contents of this body shop had been attached for public auction.

The three hostages stepped slowly inside, keenly aware of Shockley's Magnum at their backs.

The dim light of the sodden day seeped through dirt-streaked windows to cast a pale illumination on the cluttered room. Ben noted with satisfaction that here were all the equipment and raw materials he'd need. Though what he had in mind was a job he'd never seen done before.

"This what you were after?" asked the man who had volunteered his familiarity with the area.

"This'll do just fine." Ben waved his gun toward a rack of sheet-metal. "Those sheets of quarter-inch go inside the bus. And we'll need those angle-irons for support."

Mally watched as the three hostages set to work, two loading the metal while the third grappled with an oxyacetylene welding rig. Unconsciously, she twined her arm around Ben's and laced her fingers with his. From the moment they'd walked out of the motel room together, she hadn't allowed herself to doubt the successful conclusion of their plan. Indeed, she now found herself thinking of everything as *theirs.* And that included Ben's infectious confidence. The hijacking had been almost a lark, but as the heavy sheets of metal scraped past her along the floor, an ominous vision of what was to come began to settle in her imagination. And try as she might, she couldn't completely dispel the fear that crept into her.

Ben slid his arm free. "I've gotta help get this job moving."

"Then I will, too!" she said, and grabbed an end of one of the metal sheets.

"Get your ass up here!" Blakelock gripped his phone with the white-knuckled tautness of a man whose options were running out fast.

"That's impossible, sir. We mustn't be seen together." As usual, Feyderspiel spoke with icy conviction.

"But we've got to think... talk... I mean, just how much does this Josephson know?"

"Nothing that can hurt us. Yet. He's not certain of Shockley's sanity."

"Why would Shockley give us his fucking route?"

"I haven't had time to melt it down," Feyderspiel answered evenly. "Perhaps some hero instinct."

"A ruse... a ploy. He's trying to manipulate us. I never figured him for—"

"As a matter of fact, my guess is that he's on the level—that's his style, as you know, straight ahead like a bull. I'll call you again as soon as I can."

"You do that, lawyer!" Blakelock's voice was a rumbling growl; his tortured vocal cords vibrated like a warped bass fiddle. "You do that, before the whole bucket blows up in our faces! Get the trial adjourned! Have a goddamned heart attack! Perjure yourself! But just get your ass up to this office! Shockley's gotta be stopped. Stopped *hard.*"

He slammed the phone down and felt the burning pain of his ulcer spreading through his stomach. Whores, ulcers, and dedicated cops. He hated them in that order. It just wasn't fair, he thought bitterly, that a man in his position should have to put up with shit like all this.

The storm had dwindled to a fine, wind-driven mist.

Shockley extinguished the blue flame of the torch, flipped up the heavy welder's mask, and stepped back to admire his handiwork.

He'd had, during his high school years, two consecutive semesters of metal shop. At the time, he'd considered them little more than a welcome escape from the tedium of the academic classroom. But at least he'd learned something from his instructor, a crusty old character who kept order with the threat of a hot torch up your ass—and one memorable afternoon, when somebody welded the shop door shut, the old man had come damn close to keeping his word.

"If the motor don't crap out on you," one of the hostages said, "a contraption like that, like that bus is now, ought to get you through World War Three."

After their initial nervousness, the three hostages had dived into their work as if enjoying a Boy Scout project, and the job was finished quicker than Ben had expected.

The fortification was crude, but promisingly sound. A turret of sheet-metal enclosed the upper half of the driver's seat on all four sides. There were a few inches of clear between the roof and the top of the turret; there was a crawl-space at the bottom, and a small cutaway slit for his eyes.

From any outside vantage point, he would be completely enclosed as he drove.

He was aware of Mally standing beside him. "What do you think?"

Her eyes moved from him to the turret and back again. "I think you're crazy, of course." She smiled. "And I think it's time we hit the road."

Ben turned to the three hostages. "Okay, fellas, shove off."

They held their ground, wary of a trap.

"I needed your muscle," Ben told them. "Now the job's over. So walk. It's just a few blocks back to the station. Hardly raining."

"You know, mister," said the man whose wife had worried, "I don't know who you are or what your game is, and I don't know what you got planned for that war wagon, but I'll be damned if I don't hope you make it."

"Thanks." Ben smiled at him. "Sorry for the detour."

"Hell, in a way it was kind of fun. You know what I mean?"

"Yeah." His expression hardened. "Now, out, all of you! *Scram!*"

They raced for the door, shot out and away through the fog. Yes, Ben thought, he knew what the man meant. Up until that moment, there'd been an exhilaration in the design and its execution. They had worked with steel and a welding torch like they had probably always wanted to do—or at least hadn't done since they were kids.

But the fun part was over. What remained was a big, fear-some question mark.

Ben slid beneath the turret on his belly, pulled himself up to the driver's seat, and settled in. He yanked the door lever, and with a pneumatic hiss, the door swung shut.

He rapped on the side of the turret. "All set?"

"All set," Mally called back. "We blasting off straight up, or what?"

"We'll see." Ben hit the ignition and fired up the massive, rear-end diesel. He gripped the heavy gearshift, maneuvering it through its changes. Then he brought his foot down on the wide plate of the accelerator. The giant vehicle lurched unexpectedly backwards and Mally bounced hard off the turret.

"Ouch!" Then she chuckled. "Hey, this is gonna be a great trip."

She could feel his eyes glaring at her through the slit in the quarter-inch steel.

"Hold on."

Struggling not to laugh, she moved to a seat, heard the grind of gears, and suddenly felt the bus move smoothly ahead. They were on their way.

A Greyhound Scenicruiser is not a tank. But it is not exactly a kiddie car. It is eleven feet tall, eight feet wide, forty feet long, and weighs fourteen tons. It has three axles, eight size 22.5 heavy-duty tires, extra-thick shatterproof glass windows, and it is made to stand up for a million miles of service. It has a mammoth diesel engine housed at the rear behind heavy alloy siding. A Scenicruiser simply does not break down.

Add to the standard model Shockley's homemade turret.

Then it might as well be a tank.

The Scenicruiser surged down the highway, parting the condensation that rose from the warming asphalt in billows of eerie fog.

CHAPTER 25

The word traveled fast, just as Shockley had predicted. It went from the bus driver to Greyhound headquarters, from there to the Kingman police then to the Phoenix P.D., and onto Lieutenant Commander Blakelock: Detective Ben Shockley, for whom an all-points-bulletin had been issued, had apparently hijacked a bus and was headed for Phoenix.

Court was adjourned for the day, and Feyderspiel stood patiently in a public phone booth, listening to the guttural ramblings of Commander Blakelock.

"Kingman… Phoenix… Two hundred miles of goddam desert… four hours on that road." Blakelock's mangled voice was heavy with desperation. "We could, aaah, blast that bus to hell… sitting duck, you know? Call Vegas… the boys… have them do it… blow the shit out of it."

"I could make the call, sir," Feyderspiel said calmly, "but it wouldn't do us any good. They wouldn't do it. A job like that —well, let's just say it carries much too high a profile."

"What the hell! Are they with us or against us?"

Feyderspiel shook his head and looked at the ceiling of the booth. Handling Blakelock was sometimes like dealing with a petulant child. Blakelock, in Feyderspiel's opinion, had already mucked up the job by paying scant attention to certain small details—as in the selection of Shockley, for instance. Blakelock didn't have a strong sense of judgment. The ability to see, for example, that Shockley was a good deal more durable than had been thought. And now the commander seemed unable to grasp the continuing requirements for discretion: subtlety, tact, and precision—all Feyderspiel's strong points. The stakes were exceedingly high, and Blackelock could blow it all with his hysterical bumbling.

"Try to understand, sir," Feyderspiel said calmly, "we're talking about a Greyhound bus on a well-traveled public highway. Were something to happen to it out there, out of our jurisdiction, we would not have a prayer of controlling the fallout. That would be bound to be big news, and our friends in Las Vegas get rather embarrassed by that kind of coverage."

"Well, then," Blakelock shot back, "how about *our* boys? Deputy Sheriffs. Highway Patrol..." He rattled off the list with a total lack of concern for the various jurisdictions. "We've got heavy weapons, don't we? Bazookas... have the assholes show some balls... blow him away!"

Feyderspiel sighed. Clearly, he wasn't getting through to Blakelock. "With all respect, sir, there'd be too many people caught in the middle. Think about it. We don't want blood and tennis rackets all over the asphalt, do we?"

"Screw it! A few casualties—"

"Listen!" Feyderspiel interrupted, speaking more firmly now. "Casualties have to be explained, justified. If there are *any* casualties other than Shockley and the girl, someone will be answerable. And that someone is *you.* Am I correct?"

Blakelock growled.

"Sir, am I getting through to you? After all, I'm just as anxious to get the job done as you are. But it is pointless to accomplish it in such a way as to destroy us with it. I'm trying to protect you, sir—to protect us."

There was a long pause before Blakelock growled, "Are there any other options?"

Feyderspiel had him at last. But he knew enough not to be over-anxious with his advantage, or Blakelock might easily take things back into his own clumsy but potent hands. "I suggest, sir, that we let Shockley drive right into the city. After all, we have his route."

"Go on," Blakelock mumbled.

"We employ a two-phase plan. First we use his friend, Josephson, to gain his confidence. Phase two consists of clearing the streets along his route, deploying our men, creating an impossible barrier—a gauntlet, if you will. I guarantee you he won't have a chance, and our problems will be over. What I am suggesting affords us—you—total control over the entire matter."

Blakelock's answer came quickly. "That would work, sure. I mean, we could control the media then, too. We'd appear justified, getting him that way... lunatic rogue cop in a hijacked bus like destroying a wild grizzly... it would even be a feather in our caps."

"Excellent thinking, sir." In the phone booth, Feyderspiel smiled to himself.

"Then that's the plan. You work out the details, I'll run it. Can you handle... arrange the thing with this Josephson?"

"Don't worry about Josephson. I've already got him under control. I'll put it in the works right away."

"Do that. Yes. I'll run the show from here. Battalion captains... everybody will be taking their orders from my office, and my office only."

"Of course. You'll be in total command. In the meantime, perhaps you can jot down some thoughts on the matter."

"Thoughts?"

Feyderspiel chuckled at the irony of it all. "For the six o'clock news. Let's face it, Commander, in a few hours from now you're going to be a very big celebrity."

An animal grunt of satisfaction came across the line.

"Goodbye, sir," Feyderspiel said smoothly. He replaced the receiver gently in its cradle and kissed his fingers.

CHAPTER 26

Sunlight streamed through the fresh, rain-washed air, pierced the vast tinted windshield of the Scenicruiser, and gleamed on the metal turret.

Mally occupied an aisle seat two rows behind Ben. Her seat was in the recline position, and her tired body had adjusted to the smooth rumble of the bus along the highway. For a while she imagined herself on a pleasant trip to a vacation spa. But the reverie didn't last.

"Ben? What do you think they'll do to us?"

"Whatever Blakelock tells them." He was glad she couldn't see the tight lines of worry that etched his face.

"And he's sick."

"Not one of your gentle philosophers, that's true."

"Isn't there somebody who can stop him? The chief? The commissioner?"

"They could, but they won't."

"Why the hell not?"

"Blakelock's head of Internal Affairs. They're the watchdog of the department, the sacred cows of the system. That makes him one very big man. Whatever he says, they'll believe. He could put an army on the streets and nobody'd ask him why. He doesn't have to give reasons. Internal security, that's all he has to say."

"All that power in one man." She squirmed in her seat, trying to forget her meeting with him. "It's absurd."

"No more than anything else in life."

She closed her eyes. Ben was such a contradictory mixture, unshakable confidence and optimism on the one hand, deep cynicism on the other. Absurdities seemed part and parcel of her own existence. After all, she thought, here she was riding a hijacked bus right into the middle of God-only-knows-what with an avenging angel by the name of Shockley who used a Magnum as casually as most people used a cigarette lighter, and who, believe it or not, she'd managed to fall one hundred percent in love with. If she could trust such an emotional concept after all these years. If she had any sense—but what was the use? She was stuck, skewered by her own feelings, a walking, talking, love-struck fool who didn't even know if she'd be alive the next time the sun came up.

"You do want kids, don't you?" she asked wistfully.

Shockley's eyes were fixed through the turret's slit on the open highway, but the answer came without any hesitation.

"Kids, house, car, swimming pool, mortgage, groceries, bills, dog—the works."

She smiled. It was easy like this—she with her eyes closed, he behind his fortification. They were detached. Their intimacy was still tentative in many ways. "Someplace with trees?" she asked. "Someplace not with neighbors right next door? With hills to walk in?"

"Horses," he responded. "A greenhouse."

"And maybe a little guest house in back, for our friends, far enough away so we'd still have our privacy. Maybe even…"

She was aware suddenly of the unreality of her dream. "Maybe what?"

"Nothing," she said, and opened her eyes. "Hell, you don't even know if I'm good in bed."

"Don't worry. I'll take it on faith."

City Hall was a brooding eminence, a monument to mediocrity and bureaucracy.

From it, an hour from now, on a normal day, would begin the exodus of workers making their weary way homeward through the crowded streets.

But today was no normal day.

Squad cars moved in formation along the broad approach avenue, peeling off in pairs to block side streets. Uniformed officers deployed to redirect traffic. A municipal truck advanced from intersection to intersection, lowering red and yellow roadblock standards equipped with battery-powered, yellow-flashing lights. It was all conducted with military efficiency, and all the movement was overlaid with the sound of blaring car horns as angry motorists found their progress mysteriously impeded.

"Clear this street," an officer's voice boomed from the loud-hailer of a slowly cruising squad car. "This is a police emergency. All pedestrians will clear the street immediately. Clear the street under penalty of arrest. This is a police emergency..."

The clearing procedure and instructions were repeated on each street that touched on Ben's promised direct route to City Hall.

High up in the Hall, Blakelock watched from his office window as the gauntlet took shape. The meaning of the word "Commander" in his title came home to him now. He'd mobilized a strike force of awesome proportions—scores of men jumping to his bidding, faithful, well-trained, ready to kill on command. On *his* command. His men were ready to wipe two pawns off the board and go home to their families and girlfriends and beer, no questions asked.

No questions asked of him, at least. It was going to be one hell of a sight to see, all right. But no matter how much he relished the thought of what was to come, his anticipation was tempered with a trace of apprehension. Shockley had proven to be one lucky son of a bitch. He'd been the perfect candidate for the assignment except for one thing: he was still alive.

That bastard Shockley, that colorless, undistinguished cop, had simply put his head down and plowed through.

And now he had something much more dangerous than luck going for him. He had desire—the desire to crucify Lieutenant Commander Edgar G. Blakelock.

Lots of cops resented Blakelock's unquestioned power; that was common in any department that had an internal affairs division. But it was infuriating that this one lackluster, bull-headed cop could cause him so much grief.

Could cause him—he hated to admit it—even to be a bit afraid.

Blakelock walked back to his desk and sank heavily into his leather swivel chair. Maybe, he thought ruefully, he should have pulled the trigger on Augustina Mally when he had the chance.

The recollection of that incident gave him a brief, erotic twinge.

"Gus?"

"Hmmm?" Mally roused herself at his unusual use of her nickname.

Within the turret, Ben shifted in the driver's seat, regretting that he'd ever opened his mouth. But now he had to go on. "You said you've got a college degree."

"That's right. I do." She wondered where he was headed with that, if he was going to probe her discomforting past.

"Well, then... I mean how... shit, what I'm trying to say is, when our grandchildren ask me how Grams got to be a hooker, what do I tell the little bastards?"

"Tell them to watch their smart mouths."

"Yeah. I was out of line there. Sorry. Let's forget the whole thing."

She took off her shoe and tossed it at the turret. The resounding, unexpected clang made him jump. "Hey! What the hell!"

"Take it easy, Shockley. I just wanted to make sure that steel plate was *around* your head and not *in* it."

As much as it distressed her, caused her even to tremble at the thought of it, she wanted to share her life with him as he had shared his with her. This was not the best of places or the best of times—not hollering through the turret as they headed toward a fearsome confrontation with an entire police department. But, on the other hand, it might be the only place and time. There might never be another chance for her to tell it, not to anyone.

"So are you ready for my autobiography or not?" she said finally.

"Ask a simple question—"

"And you'll get a simple answer, more or less." Mally kicked off her other shoe and tucked her feet up beneath her.

"I was in New York City, sharing an apartment with an equally out-of-work girlfriend, my precious B.A. degree neatly framed and hanging on the wall. She had one, too, by the way, and we were both out to beat the world. Beat it with our liberal-arts smarts. Well, we looked and we looked and we looked, and the only thing our degrees netted us was a few dinner invitations and some very uninspiring propositions that we immediately turned down as soon as the check was paid. I mean, after all, women's lib will out, right? Wrong.

"Between the two of us we were making about as much headway as the anemic goldfish we kept in a bowl, constantly swimming around in circles and running into the glass."

"Didn't you have a guy or—"

"Shut up, will you? Let me tell it." She took a few breaths.

"So one night I was in this singles bar, crying in my beer, and this guy came up and made the mistake of asking me what was wrong. Well, his timing couldn't have been better, and I unloaded the whole sad story on him. Not including, by the way, the fact that I didn't know if I had a boyfriend or not, because he went off to Vietnam and I never heard from him again. I guess I loved the dumb son of a bitch.

"So I told this guy about how tough it was. I felt like a fool all the time while I was doing it, but somehow I got the feeling he really sympathized with me.

"Anyway, he took me home, and I found out why he'd been such a good listener. It seems he was a baseball player, a big name who hadn't had the sense to quit while he was ahead. He knew what hard times were all about. He'd had them once and could see them coming up again. But that didn't stop him from leaving the two hundred dollars I found when I woke up the next morning.

"Later he brought me to Vegas during spring training. But they cut him from the team, and he just disappeared. My guys always seem to be doing that, don't they? Except for you, and you're stuck with me.

"So anyway, he split, and by then I'd given up kidding myself about a career or a decent job or making any money in normal ways. So I just stayed on, in Vegas..."

Men were so easy. They were a snap. All Gus Mally had to do

was twitch her neat, round butt and they'd come running to her, panting and stumbling all over themselves.

They took her to dinner and shows, and gave her all-around good times. All she had to do was be willing and warm. Not that the sex was all bad—not by a long shot.

Quite often she really enjoyed it—with certain men, at certain times. But it was all so foolish and transparent, the whole song and dance. Sometimes she almost found herself saying: Let's go to bed first. Then if we still want to go to dinner and a show, fine, I'd enjoy it. And I'd feel better about it. And incidentally, I might just find somebody to fall in love with, if we went about it that way, went about it honestly.

Mally's best friend was Ginger, a pretty and vivacious blonde like Mally. For a while they shared a nice, two-bedroom apartment near the Strip. Ginger had money, plenty of it.

Mally assumed it was family money, because, unlike Mally, Ginger didn't have a job. She wasn't stingy; she paid most of the rent and most of the bills, and bought most of the groceries. Mally contributed what she could from her earnings as secretary to a travel agent.

They both dated a lot, virtually every night, but almost never together. Ginger preferred to be alone with her dates, thought it less of a strain on their relationship, and that was fine with Mally.

Sleepover dates were not uncommon, though usually they went to their men's places. And when they both had sleepovers in their own apartment, it was no hassle. Ginger's date was usually gone by the time Mally got up.

The only thing Mally fretted about was money. Having Ginger pay the freight made Mally uncomfortable.

One morning she voiced it. "Gin, I just don't want you paying for my stuff any more. I feel so small. It's not fair to either of us. I'm a grown woman, and I should be taking care of myself."

Ginger slowly stirred her coffee. "As far as me paying, it doesn't bother me at all—you know that, hon. But as far as what you're saying goes, I can dig it. I can see how it would bother you. The point is"—she smiled down at her coffee—"there's just no need for you to be in hock all the time."

"Gin, I just can't find a better job. I look all the time. There's nothing—"

"Your job should be *you,* hon. Just like my job is me."

"Your job?"

"I learned a long time ago, Gus, that I don't have to be *giving* it away. There's as much market for *me* out there as there is for any slot machine." She chuckled at the analogy.

"What are you saying?" Mally stared at her.

"What I'm saying is, being taken to dinners and shows is not profit. The profit is *there"*—she waved toward her room—"on the bed."

"You don't mean..."

"Come on, Gus, you're not so innocent. Yeah, my men pay, most of them. What the hell, I enjoy a good lover. So do you. Are you so much into the Puritan work ethic that work has to be a drudgery? Don't you think anybody has work that they really *love* to do? Well, I love my work, which is love, to use the common euphemism. Shocked?"

"I am, frankly."

"Where in blazes did you think I got my money?"

"To be truthful, I thought it was in your family, or something."

"It's in my sweet box, hon, to be crude about it." Ginger smiled.

"Jesus, Gin, that's practically being a *hooker."*

"It's *precisely* being a hooker. I have no illusions about it. But I do it in a much nicer way, much pleasanter way, than most. Almost every guy I date is a guy I *want* to date. I don't prowl the streets picking up uglies. I don't have anybody telling me *who* to date. We have a good time, a few laughs, some talk, some hand-holding—everything is just as nice and pleasant and friendly as the real thing. Except there's an agreement beforehand. The agreement is that we'll end up in bed, and I'll be paid. It's that simple. Why are you frowning?"

"I'm just trying to take it all in." Mally shook her head. "It's so strange, so *unreal.*"

"What's unreal about it? It's a hell of a lot more real and healthy than most of the so-called 'normal' boy-girl bull shit. You've said it yourself, Gus, We've talked about it, about how you sometimes would like to just screw the guy first thing, and then go ahead and enjoy an evening out on the town together if you both feel like it. You've said it would be so much more *honest* that way. Well, my way is totally honest. No bullshit. I like a guy, I go out with him. It's just that we know beforehand exactly what's involved."

"You *always* like the guy?" Mally put her chin in her hands and stared.

Ginger shrugged. "Most of the time. Sometimes, like when the rent's due or something, I may bend my standards a little. But what the hell, did you always want to fuck every guy you fucked?"

"I guess so."

"Well, then, you're unusual."

"Can I ask you..." Mally took a deep breath. "What do you... um... charge?"

Ginger smiled. "It depends. I'm not greedy. If the guy's loaded, and most of them *are* around here, maybe two. If he's not, I'll settle for one. Never less than that. They wouldn't respect me."

"Hundred?"

"Yeah."

"Jesus!"

"It's good. *I'm* good. You'll be good, too."

"I couldn't."

"Do me a favor, do yourself a favor—try it. First couple of

times you'll be a little nervous. But then you'll relax and enjoy."

"Ooof!" Mally grimaced.

"Listen!" Ginger leaned over the table, her expression turning serious. "To start you out, I'll fix you up, set up the dates for you. I'll bring the guys here first, you can look them over, get to know them, choose the ones you want. I'll set the price and everything. All you have to do is... well"—she chuckled—"make love. I don't mind sharing with you. After all, it'll take some of the weight off my pocketbook."

"Jesus."

"Our only bargain is that you'll try it. You owe me that much. Okay?"

Mally's head swirled; she didn't know what was going on, and she didn't know what she was being told, and she didn't know what she was saying.

"Okay." She looked up at Ginger. "Okay."

"Smile."

Mally smiled.

"Laugh."

Mally roared with the craziness of it all.

Mally stared out of the bus window, squinting into the late-afternoon sun. "Well, the first few dates were pretty much like she said. I tried to enjoy them, but I couldn't really. But I made a bundle. So I quit my job right away. We moved out of the apartment and rented that house I took you to, the one they blew up on us. The neighborhood wasn't quite as bad then, and we had plans to fix the place up and all, make it really like a nice home.

"But then gradually Ginger's clientele began to change. I didn't notice it at first. But some heavies started coming around —you know, syndicate types. I don't know who they were. She got involved with them somehow, and some shit came down, and she all of a sudden had to do a disappearing act. I don't know where she went. But there I was, alone with our marvelous business, and I didn't know what the hell was going on.

"Well, then the syndicate guys started coming around to see *me.* Same guys, expecting the same treatment. I tried to avoid them, but I couldn't. I even looked for a job, looked for a guy to fall in love with—everything. They threatened me, locked me in, started ordering me around. They said if I didn't play ball, they'd cut off my tits and tie me out in the desert where the sun could heal me real quick."

Mally gritted her teeth. "Real bastards. They gave me a job, supposed to go see some john in a hotel. I refused. Next thing I knew, I was busted for being a hooker. So I was hooked, all right. They had me. They got me out of the slam, and then they knocked me around for a while. Then they turned me out. Yup. They gave me dates; I went to hotels and motels, split the money—the works. I was a bonafide, true-life, genuine lady of the night.

"You better be listening, Shockley, cause this is a one-time performance!"

"I'm listening."

"I never knew anything about their business, didn't *want* to know. Then this guy DeLucca came along, Little Angel. He was one of them I hadn't seen before. He wanted a piece of ass. I told him to go fuck himself. He was little, like his name. I mean a nobody. He just wanted a quickie before he sent me out on this job he had for me. I told him to jack off. I went on the job. The job was Blakelock.

"But I guess Little Angel got tired of being little, because the next thing I know, he's in Phoenix, Arizona, running his mouth.

"And that, Mister Ben Shockley, is about where you come in. All I know is, one night the cops roust me without a warrant or a charge, lock me up, and then I meet this crazy cop who asked me to take a bus ride with him."

The bus rolled to a stop on the shoulder of the highway.

"The bus ride's over," Ben said.

Mally remained in her seat, staring at the metal turret. "I thought we'd been through all that."

The door swung open, admitting the hot desert air.

"Crawl out of your bunker, Shockley," she said.

"Just go. Don't make it any harder than it already is."

"Sorry, I don't take orders from faceless voices."

Ben slid out from beneath the turret. The idling monster diesel vibrated the bus around them.

"Now tell me again," Mally said coldly. "Tell me you want to call off the relationship."

"That's not what I said."

"It amounts to the same thing."

"If I come out the other end of this alive, we can pick up where we left off."

"Like hell. Either we've got a marriage in the works here or we haven't. That's all I want to know."

He reached out to take her hand, but she withheld it. "You haven't answered my question yet."

He wished he could tell her he didn't love her. He wished he could throw her bodily off the bus and slam the door. But he realized it was impossible for *anything* to come between them, even a suicide mission in a hijacked bus.

"Sorry for the pit stop," he said.

Then she took his hand and lightly brushed the back of it with her lips. "Apology accepted. Now get your ass back in the driver's seat. The quicker we get to City Hall, the quicker we can start our life."

Ben wormed back into the turret.

"Hey, Shockley, maybe while we're there we can pick up the license!" Mally said.

. . .

Josie's life was unreeling in his head with unprecedented clarity, but he wasn't dying. He was in his parked squad car, alone. Behind him, the massive network of roadblocks kept people and traffic from the streets. Curving up and away before him was the off-ramp Ben would be using for his entrance into the city. What had happened to Josie was that he had finally put the last piece of the puzzle into place.

The realization had dawned on him with brutal force, right after his last meeting with Feyderspiel, and try as he might, Josie had been unable to shake the undeniable facts from his mind.

He'd been set up. Just as surely as Ben had been set up, and just as subtly. Only it had been done to him by condeming him to life behind a desk instead of death in the desert. It was a realization all the more powerful for its late arrival, and Josie was clouded with shame as he relived his family's congratulations, their looks of pride, the intimate dinner with his wife.

Despite his protestations, he'd been damn pleased with the promotion. His years of hard work had been recognized.

He'd fancied himself a man finally rewarded—when in fact, he realized now, he'd been a manipulated fool, an obstruction on the landscape that had been casually kicked out of the way. Kicked out of the way so that he wouldn't interfere with the track of the bullet that was heading for his partner.

It was a dose of reality as bitter as aspirin. Christ, he thought angrily, he'd actually *liked* his work. He was not like so many of the guys who wandered into the force because it was as good a place as any to put in their time, collect their pensions, and see some excitement along the way. Cleaning up the streets had *meant* something to him. He didn't give a damn about the discounts from the merchants, the offers of late-night freebies from the whores. Sure, they'd all been there for the taking, but that wasn't why he was a cop. Not that he passed judgment on the guys who took advantage of what was offered; that was their business. He and Ben were similar in that attitude. What he was after was the garbage—the rapists, the pushers, the muggers who grabbed a purse and then kicked in a kidney just for good measure.

That's what he was all about, that's what he'd laid his life on the line for more times than he could remember. And what had it gotten him? A supporting role in a neat little production to annihilate one of the few good friends he had.

His best friend. And he'd fallen in step with all the naiveté of the village idiot. Jesus, what a climax to a career! Maynard Josephson, first-class schmuck!

Josie slammed the heel of his hand against the steering wheel. When he got the word on Blakelock, he should've gone up and thrown him out of his goddam twelfth-story window. From the beginning Ben had been wary of all that power in one individual, and he'd been right. Blakelock was king of his own private world, and he didn't give a shit what he did to secure his position.

Josie tried to calm himself. He had a job to do, perhaps the most important of his life. He had to convince Ben that there was a way out, a way they could nail Blakelock and open up an investigation that would flush the department of all the filth, no matter how far up it went.

But it wasn't going to be easy. He knew what Ben was like when he was after someone.

Still, they had a friend, a man with the power of the law behind him. A man who was clean, tough, and ambitious enough to take the risk. A man that was smart enough to twist Blakelock into a pretzel on the witness stand. Through this man, they'd get Blakelock. The only way. He had to make Ben see that. Had to make him understand that they could trust John Feyderspiel, Assistant D.A.

CHAPTER 27

"Supposing he gets through?" Blakelock's voice croaked across the line.

Feyderspiel was getting disgusted with the man's fits of panic and doubt. "He can't get through. How many units have you deployed? Four dozen? Five?" Feyderspiel knew exactly how many.

"Yeah, yeah, I know. But there'll be hell to pay if something goes wrong."

"The only thing that could possibly go wrong is if your spit-and-polish disciples suddenly decide they can't shoot down a fellow officer."

"They're cops. Stupid slaves. The bastards are paid to shoot, not think."

"Then we have no problem," Feyderspiel said.

The downtown interchange loomed in front of Ben, a graceful, swooping network of reinforced concrete. Traffic was rapidly slowing, and as he rounded a curve he saw why: flares burning brightly in the pale dusk; a police roadblock funneling the four lanes of rush-hour motorists away from the downtown artery that was the first leg of Ben's pre-announced route.

Mally had been in a restless half-sleep when the slowing of the bus awakened her. "What's the matter?" she asked, blinking.

"Roadblock."As Ben spoke, he twisted the oversized steering wheel to the right, slid between a pair of astonished drivers, and headed the Scenicruiser directly at the wooden barriers.

Mally gripped the arm of her seat as the bus picked up speed. Suddenly everything she had thought about was going to happen; the future had become the present, and she didn't know what to do.

"Hit the deck!" Ben shouted.

She threw herself to the floor, her head buried in her arms, her nails digging into the palms of her tightly clenched hands.

Like a roaring tank, the bus thundered along the vacant approach to the fragile barricades of the connecting ramp.

Ben envisioned the crash of splintering wood, and his right hand instinctively moved to his Magnum.

But nothing happened. One of the uniformed officers stepped calmly forward and waved the bus through, but Ben noted in the rear-view mirror that the temporary opening was quickly sealed behind them.

Mally cautiously raised her head, startled by the absence of any impact. "They let us through?"

"Blakelock's covering himself from all angles. He doesn't want any innocent people hurt. Have a look."

She stood up and saw the empty, curving stretch of freeway before them.

"The bottom of *that* is where our welcoming committee's going to greet us," Ben said grimly.

"What will they do?"

"Who knows?"

"Couldn't we just keep going?" Mally spoke rapidly, afraid to let herself think about what she was saying. "Maybe they'd never stop us. Maybe we could just go away, and—"

"Nag, nag, nag." His voice was a gentle tug back to reality, and she slumped in her seat.

"It's not fair," she said quietly. "We never even had a goddam honeymoon."

Josie kept his solitary vigil at the foot of the off-ramp, a shabby urban capillary shadowed by soot-blackened buildings. The long wait had been a harsh ordeal of self-revelation for him, and his anger had finally turned to impatience. Then he heard a distant sound that quickly grew into the full-blown rumble of a highballing diesel. He looked up to see the silver Scenicruiser crest the ramp and nose down the incline, heading straight for him.

He stepped from the black-and-white, waving his arms in greeting, and hoping to hell Ben would recognize him in time to stop that big hearse of his.

Mally eyed the waving figure through the right half of the huge windshield. "What's that all about?"

Ben eased up on the gas. "It's Josie."

"Who?"

"My partner for the last fifteen years."

"Then we can trust him."

"If I didn't think so, I'd run him the hell over."

Josie held his ground as the big machine rolled to a hissing stop a few feet from his squad car. Hesitantly, he crossed to the idling bus. The door swung open and he mounted the steps. He was immediately confronted by Shockley, who stood next to his makeshift turret.

"Jeeesus, Ben! You look like you're going to war!"

"I am. What's up? What are you doing here?"

Josie gave a cursory glance at Mally, then plunged ahead.

"Look, you don't have to go through all this. We've got a friend at City Hall. You're gonna be safe."

"Who?" The single word left no doubt of Ben's suspicions.

"John Feyderspiel. You know him?"

"I've seen him around. Fair-haired boy in the D.A.'s office."

"Right But what's more important, he's also the prosecutor on the DeLucca case. I told him what you said about Blakelock. He took it in like a pro, Ben. He's a tough son of a bitch. Believe me, he's got no axe to grind one way or the other. He ain't afraid of Blakelock one bit—I'm not even sure he respects him all that much. He said he'd personally represent you if you can prove your point."

"Forget it. I don't trust anybody connected with the DeLucca case."

"Dammit, didn't you hear me? He's the prosecutor!" Josie was beginning to sweat.

"Ben!" Mally put her hand on his arm. "Maybe he's the one." Her voice was tinged with hope. "Maybe the one person with the guts to go up against Blakelock."

"And maybe they're in bed together!" Ben snarled. "Maybe the whole thing's rigged—prepare the case, blow it, forget it. The whole trial could be a fucking smokescreen!"

"Ben, listen to me," Josie urged. "I know how you feel. At this point you probably think the whole department's crooked, and for all I know, maybe they are. But at least this way we can find out. So trust me. I talked to Feyderspiel. He's okay. He's smart and he's cool. Take my word for it. Besides, you really don't have any choice. Blakelock's got half the force out there waiting for his silver elephant to roll down the street."

"Where?"

"The whole route you gave me. The place is swarming

with black-and-whites." Josie waved impatiently at the turret. "Hell, even with this pig-iron, it's suicide. Please.

Transfer to my car. Stay low in back. I'll smuggle you into City Hall. Feyderspiel and I have it all doped out. We take the service elevator to his office. He says to keep your gun. Says if you think you're being crossed you can use him as your hostage. What more can you ask, for chrissake? The guy's laying his life on the line for you!"

Josie's sincerity was convincing. Ben wanted to get Blakelock, but he also wanted to be alive when it was finished, and the main reason for that desire to live was standing right next to him.

"What do you think?" he asked Mally.

She was scared, and she knew it showed; her answer didn't come quickly. "I think it's worth a try," she said finally.

Ben let out a long, slow breath. "Okay." He turned to his old partner. "Josie, say hello to Gus Mally."

Josie held out a ham-sized hand and cracked his spare parts face in a broad smile. "Come on, let's go."

Leaving the engine still idling, the three of them stepped from the bus. A draft of stale air whipped a cellophane wrapper across their path. The street was deserted, but above them, where they could not see, there was life.

Steadily, quietly, with careful professional efficiency, a pair of marksmen dressed in the olive fatigues of a special tactical unit shifted their positions on an overlooking rooftop and sighted their targets.

Josie followed Mally and Ben to his black-and-white.

The marksmen above held their rifles still, fingers firmly against the triggers.

When they reached the car, Josie stepped suddenly around Ben, meaning to open the door for Mally.

Just then, the marksmen fired.

The sharp pops of rifle fire shattered the stillness, and the bullets meant for Ben ripped into Josie instead. He twitched several times from the unseen blows, and then his riddled body toppled into Ben's outstretched arms.

"The bus!" The command tore from Ben's throat.

Mally dashed for the open door of the bus. Ben struggled with Josie's ungainly body, unwilling to accept the death of his friend, unwilling to leave him there.

He dragged Josie across the road toward the bus, more bullets glancing off the concrete around him, some thudding into Josie's corpse. From the safety of the bus, Mally heard his gasp in pain as a ricochet tore the calf of his leg and brought him to his knees only a few paces away.

She hurled herself out at him. Her fists pummeled his back, and she screamed for him to let Josie go. "He's dead!

Leave him, Ben! He was trying to *save* you! He wouldn't want to cause you to die with him! He's dead!" She pulled him toward the cover of the bus, away from Josie's lifeless form.

Bullets spattered around them. For one terrible moment, Mally thought that Ben would rush back into the line of fire.

Then he whirled, dived through the open door into the bus and into his turret.

She clambered into the bus behind him and huddled beside the steel plating of his fortification. The door slammed shut.

"They killed him!" Ben raged. "The sons of bitches killed him! Fucking punks! It was Feyderspiel! Feyderspiel and Blakelock!"

Grinding the gearshift into low, he wrenched the big steering wheel to the left and slapped his foot down on the gas. The mighty tires revolved, and, like a ship setting out to sea, the huge bus whined onto the deserted city streets.

From their rooftop, the marksmen peppered the bus with round after round. But it didn't slow. It absorbed the attack, seemed to gather momentum, and lumbered out of range.

"You okay?" Ben's voice was as cold as the steel that enclosed him.

Mally swallowed hard. "Yeah. I think so. What about your leg?"

"To hell with my leg. Just hold on tight, lady. We're going in!"

He swerved the bus around a corner to his left and plowed ahead down the middle of the vacant, gaping street.

CHAPTER 28

The cement corridor stretched in front of them, barren of traffic, more lifeless than the desert. But Ben knew that the very things he didn't see were the things he had to fear.

Josie's words echoed in his racing thoughts: Blakelock's got half the force out there, waiting...

And it was the truth.

Men were hidden along the entire north side of the street, in every doorway, every place of concealment, every niche large enough to contain a human being—a firing line of awesome proportions. Rifles, shotguns, Magnums, all were at the ready.

As the sound of the charging diesel trumpeted down the street, a battalion captain stiffly raised a bullhorn to his mouth, trying to divorce himself from the fact that he was about to give the order to cut down a fellow officer. But there was nothing he could do about it, short of gross insubordination. Blakelock was the boss, and he must know what he was doing. Must know...

. . .

Inside the bus, Ben held the wheel in a sweaty, vice-like grip. Instinct told him that major violence was near. "It's gonna bust loose any second now," he yelled. "Grab the floor!"

Mally flattened herself in the aisle, an arm's length from the turret. She wanted to be near him when they died.

"Open fire!"

The amplified voice boomed above the roar of the engine and was answered by Ben with a brazen challenge from the bus horn. Then both sounds were drowned out by a cannonade of gunfire.

Traveling at sixty miles an hour, the Scenicruiser was fourteen tons of charging bull elephant, and it absorbed the impact of the first rounds without slowing down.

Bullets shattered windows, ripped into empty seats, splattered off Shockley's turret and the metal interior of the bus, whining and ricocheting like swarms of deadly insects gone mad. The noise alone was numbing to Ben and Mally, but the fear it brought with it was worse—a palpable demon that seized them and shook them to the roots of their sanity.

A deluge of hot lead slammed into Ben's turret. Mally squeezed her eyes shut against the holocaust and clamped her hands over her ears. Her body twisted as if to press itself into the very steel of the rocking, vibrating floor, her limbs contracting in involuntary spasms. She lay huddled in a fetal position, listening to the pitiful sounds of her own choking sobs, waiting for the searing pain that would bring an end.

The thundering diesel downshifted. Its throbbing engine was protected from the main thrust of the onslaught by the fact that it was in the rear and would therefore require the attackers to shoot at a tangent dangerously close to their own men. Not even Blakelock could allow his troops to risk each other in a cross-fire. His plan was only to stop Ben Shockley and the whore.

Nearing the end of the block, Ben prepared to negotiate the upcoming corner. The bombarding guns slackened off to a few random bursts, and the stunned policemen watched in amazement as the enormous gleaming bus continued to roll.

Mally felt a lurch as they rounded the corner, and then all was silent, save for the blustering engine. Unbelieving, she opened her eyes and got shakily to her knees. "Jesus... we made it!"

"Like hell we did! Geddown!"

"No!" Mally screamed it out, banging at the turret with her fists just as the remaining windows on the other side of the bus were blown inward by the new broadside of gunfire.

She dropped to the floor, cutting her arms on the broken glass. The police were on the south side this time, cratering the previously untouched flank of the bus with a hail of bullets that gouged the metal siding, ruptured the tires and, because of the oblique angle of the turn, punctured the alloy shielding around the engine.

But still the Greyhound rumbled on, steam billowing from its wounds, shredding rubber giving way to the heavy rims that scored the road with brutal scars.

And through it all, with clenched jaws, the hunters carried out their orders—Magnums bucking in their hands, rifles kicking into their shoulders, mechanically firing round after round. None of the men wanted to be the one who fired the fatal shots, or to know it if he did. All were glad they couldn't see the policeman at the wheel of the bus. One of them, a rookie, wept openly as his trigger finger jerked again and again in miserable obedience.

"Shit!" Ben's head flew back. Specks of blood popped out on his face and neck from a wild shotgun ricochet that had somehow found its way into the turret.

"Ben?"

"Shut up and keep your ass on the floor!"

Crippled but still moving, the Scenicruiser slowed as it approached an intersection where wooden barriers blocked all three avenues of escape: right, left, and dead ahead.

The barrage of gunfire dwindled from sheer lack of ammunition. Ben skidded the bus to a stop, slid from the seat and rolled out from under the turret wall, a bloody apparition that brought a stifled cry from Mally.

"Take over!" Ben barked at her.

She stared at his left leg, sodden with blood from his calf to his shoe.

"I said *drive this sucker!"* Numbed beyond recognition of what she was doing, Mally crawled beneath the turret, and then almost retched at the sight of the pool of blood that covered the accelerator pedal and glistened below it. "Oh, my Christ, Ben." Her voice was a whisper.

"Get moving!"

"I don't know how to—"

"Just do what I tell you, goddamit!" He told her how to shift the gears. "Now *go!"*

"Don't yell at me!" She pulled herself bravely upright in the seat. "Which way do I turn?"

"Left." There was a pain in his voice as he tightened his belt around his leg as a tourniquet.

She glanced left in bewilderment. "But there's a barrier that way!"

"Screw the barrier!"

Mally wrenched the gearshift suddenly as if she were going to tear it out and jammed her foot on the blood-soaked accelerator.

The bus lurched forward, so violently that Ben had to grab the arm of one of the seats to keep from sliding down the aisle, then heaved around the corner, demolishing the barrier in a crackling explosion of wood.

Hands strangling the wheel, Mally found herself headed straight down the street toward the dome of City Hall.

"Ben!"

"Yeah?"

"Christ! There's more! More cops! At the base of the stairs! Straight ahead!"

Grunting with pain, his face white from loss of blood, Ben pulled himself up on his good leg and stared grimly through the windshield.

Before the broad flight of steps leading up to City Hall stood a third battalion of police, armed and ready to defend the building.

"Ben, what do we do?" Mally yelled.

"Keep it in gear and hit the deck!"

"But—"

"Now!"

Mally heard him fall to the floor. She slid down off the seat and depressed the gas pedal with her hand just as the third assault began, a brutal stream of gunfire aimed squarely at the front of the onrushing bus.

A dying giant, the shell-pocked Scenicruiser rumbled down the street, its windshield two empty sockets, its wiper blades dangling like limp antennae. The sounds of the bus slowing were a grotesque recitation of mechanical complaints, and then, at last literally shot to death, the Greyhound gave one terminal rattle of its engine, bumped over the curb, and ground to a halt directly at the base of the wide City Hall stairs.

Only then did the hail of destruction dwindle. Another moment, and an eerie silence had fallen over the scene.

Behind the mutilated bus, the street began to fill with police—some running, some walking slowly, all giving up their positions along the gauntlet to converge on City Hall.

Guns still held at the ready, the crowd of officers gathered around the battered metal hulk of the lifeless Scenicruiser.

Gripped by tension, the blue-clad men waited. Nothing could be alive in there. It was a bullet-riddled tomb.

Then the door wheezed open. A figure appeared and descended to the first step. Ben Shockley.

Ben stood there, stained by Josie's congealed blood and by the fresh stickiness of his own. All was silence. Then somewhere in the front ranks of the crowd the hammer of a Magnum clicked back crisply. Ben lowered himself painfully down the steps. His gaunt, sunken-eyed face gazed blankly at the firepower that was trained on him.

Then he released his hold on the open door, swayed unsteadily, and turned back to the bus. He raised his hand, a gallant salute to Augustina Mally.

Gripping his hand, Mally staggered down the steps and confronted the army of guns with an almost haughty glare.

Ben's arm went protectively around her. Then he dug into his coat pocket with his free hand and extracted the bloody, tattered carbon of the subpoena.

"I'm delivering a witness," he said firmly and slowly, "to courtroom G."

Arm in arm, he and Mally moved toward the broad flight of steps. They came face to face with a seasoned policeman whose gun was leveled point-blank at Ben's chest.

"Move it," Ben said softly, "I'm going in."

The veteran didn't move. These were the people he'd been ordered to kill. He could feel the eyes of the other policemen on him, waiting for his reaction, waiting for the lead he knew somehow they'd all follow.

His eyes met Ben's.

The veteran stepped aside and let them pass.

Ben moved forward, dragging his bloodied leg. Mally and he began to mount the City Hall steps, crimson footprints marking their weaving progress.

The veteran watched them go, his gun still raised, until, in a gesture that bespoke the single mind of all those present, a battalion captain standing next to him reached out with his index finger and slowly pushed the barrel of the gun toward the ground.

Blakelock and Feyderspiel stood wavering in the lobby of City Hall. Then, in a rage of crazed frustration, Blakelock burst through the doors, screaming at the officers who lined the steps.

"Kill them! I gave orders! I *told* you! Shoot them! *Shoot to kill!*"

Feyderspiel stepped outside, stunned by the spectacle.

Ben leaped at him. He seized the attorney, pivoted him in a hammerlock, and held him at gunpoint before the shocked, silent gathering.

"Talk!" Ben spat out the word. The barrel of his Magnum at Feyderspiel's throat, he pulled the man to his tiptoes.

"Talk! Tell them!"

Panicked, his face distorted by the force of Ben's grip, Feyderspiel choked out the words: "It was... it was Blakelock... he set it up... the whole thing."

"Set up *what?"*

"The cover-up," Feyderspiel gasped.

"Cover-up of *what?"* Ben roared.

"The DeLucca trial... collusion with the underworld... he set you up... the whole thing was his idea."

The listening officers stepped back a pace, glancing at each other.

With a howl, Blakelock grabbed a pistol from a dazed policeman, whirled and fired.

Feyderspiel's body slumped. Exposed, Ben took the next shot high on his chest, and crumpled on the steps with the dead attorney.

Screaming, Mally threw herself across Ben and snatched the Magnum from his unmoving hand. Two more shots whined off the steps as Blakelock continued to fire in a blind frenzy.

Mally spun on her knees, sighted through her tears, and pulled the trigger.

Blakelock stumbled backwards, a dark stain spreading across his clean white shirt.

The blue-black Magnum bucking and thundering in her hands, Mally sent round after round ripping into Blakelock's back-pedaling figure. He staggered down the steps, still gripping his pistol. He raised it again and pulled the trigger, but the hammer fell on an empty chamber.

Mally's final shot struck him in the face, silencing forever the mangled voice that had ordered their extinction.

Dropping the gun, Mally knelt over Ben, caressing his shoulder, his cheek, his hair.

"Ben, oh God, Ben talk to me!" she wailed. "Tell me you're all right. Ben, I love you. Please... God, just tell me you're okay. Ben! *Please!*"

He lay there motionless. As she stared at his pale, battered face, the terrible fear of being alone knifed into her, and she began to shake him, shouting in despair.

"Goddamit, wake up! You hear me, Ben Shockley? Don't you die on me, you crazy bastard! You hear me? I won't let you die, you son of a bitch! Wake up! Open your fucking eyes!"

For a long moment there was no response.

Then, feebly, Ben's eyelids lifted. He glimpsed Mally's tear-streaked face through a dense fog of semiconsciousness.

"Nag, nag, nag..."

ACKNOWLEDGMENTS

Without the kindness, patience, encouragement and professional effort of three very special friends, the reissue of this book would not have been possible.

My deepest thanks and admiration go to Jim Preminger, Gary Hertz and the late Kathy Shryack

M.B.

www.ingramcontent.com/pod-product-compliance
Lightning Source LLC
La Vergne TN
LVHW030547200526
839337LV00041B/535

9781966037644